My One And Only
Bomb Shelter

My One And Only Bomb Shelter

Stories By

John Smolens

Carnegie Mellon University Press
Pittsburgh 2000

"Disciple Pigeons" first appeared in *The Massachusetts Review*, Summer 1987; "Snow" first appeared in *Yankee*, January 1989. "The Errand" first appeared in *City Limits*, January 1995; "Night Train to Chicago" appeared in *The William and Mary Review*, Spring 1999; "The Meetinghouse" appeared in *The Larcom Review*, Spring 1999; and "Cold" appeared in *Columbia*, Spring 1999.

Book and cover design: Lisa Rump and Stephen Wolfe

Library of Congress Card Catalog Number 99-074434
ISBN 0-88748-329-1 Pbk.

10 9 8 7 6 5 4 3 2 1

Stories

My One and Only Bomb Shelter
11

Cold
49

The You is Understood
71

The Errand
81

Disciple Pigeons
95

Night Train to Chicago
109

The Meetinghouse
125

Absolution
147

Snow
169

Acknowledgements:

Again and again, my thanks to
my mother
my wife Reesha
my brother Peter and his wife Linda
my sister Elizabeth and her three children
John, David and Megan
and my brother Michael.

In memory of my father
John Harrison Smolens, Sr.

To Reesha

"We don't have to live great lives, we just have to undrrstand and survive the ones we've got."

Voices from the Moon
Andre Dubus

Adios, Amigo

My One And Only
Bomb Shelter

I

It was in the part of town called Forest Glen. Every suburb of Boston has such a neighborhood, a cluster of blocks lined with houses built shortly after World War II. The streets are all named after generals and admirals. I'd stopped at every house in Forest Glen, but it was on Patton that I finally found my one and only bomb shelter.

Kevin Meehan and I actually had jobs. Pay was a dollar-sixty an hour to assist in conducting a door-to-door survey for the Commonwealth of Massachusetts. It was the summer of 1968, and most days were hot and extremely humid, causing cicadas to buzz loudly in the trees. In the morning Kevin would pick me up in his white VW bug wearing chinos and a short sleeve shirt, usually madras, sometimes striped, always freshly ironed. At orientation we had been told that proper attire was essential to conducting the survey. We carried our questionaire pad on a clipboard that bore the official state seal and we wore badges in plastic sheaths, signed by the Lieutenant Governor. We were, Kevin liked to say, B-Men.

"See Rick, you got your G-Men working for J. Edgar Hoover. They do, you know, *crime:* the rackets, narcotics, gambling, prostitution, Mob activities, you name it. But *we*—are Bomb-Shelter-Men. Da-*daah*-duh! *B-Men!* A select squad of highly-trained agents going out into the streets of America every morning, determined to protect and serve our fair citizens in the event

of nuclear attack by the Union of Soviet Socialist Republics."
Much of the time Kevin talked like a TV show. He could do this
because he hadn't played varsity sports in high school. It allowed
him to become something of a clown. I had been the goalie on
our hockey team, so it was all right for me to be the straightman.
Besides, his madras shirts were always newer, his chinos always
crisper. It was fine. We had just graduated from high school and
would enter college in the fall. In the meantime, we actually had
jobs.

•

For reasons of national security, Kevin and I spoke in code as
much as possible. We were forever vigilant because Commies
were everywhere. "I suspect," Kevin shouted over the radio one
morning as we were driving out Route 9 toward our assigned
neighborhood, "that even my bug is bugged!" We usually played
the radio loudly so that Soviet agents couldn't monitor our conversations. We blasted the music so that the dashboard of the car
vibrated to the bass of songs like "Sunshine of Your Love," "Purple
Haze" and "Respect."

Our orientation booklet said it was essential that we conduct
our mission according to strict procedure:

*Approach each dwelling only by the street. Knock or ring only at
front doors. If after ten seconds there is no response, knock or ring
once more. If after ten more seconds there is still no response, put a
circle around the street number on your survey map.*

*If a civilian answers the door, determine whether that person is an
adult living at that residence. Once you have established contact
with an adult civilian, state the following: "Hello, my name is —
— and I'm conducting a survey sanctioned by the Commonwealth of
Massachusetts to determine civilian preparedness in the case of a national emergency. Would you please permit me just a few minutes to
ask you a series of questions important to national defense?"*

*Once the civilian has agreed to the interview, proceed through the
series of questions on your form. Always ask the questions in the same*

order. Omitting questions will compromise the integrity of the survey.

Kevin and I called the survey forms dossiers. The first questions simply determined how many civilians resided in the dwelling, and their ages and gender. After the preliminary questions we asked the big one.

Does your house have a bomb shelter?

In the event that the civilian said no, we proceeded to the series of questions on the right side of the form. Should the civilian say yes, we were then to ask the questions on the left side of the form. For weeks I filled out hundreds of forms, never once getting an opportunity to fill out the left side. No one had a bomb shelter. Some said they had thought about it; some even appeared to feel guilty about not having one. Many said they had been planning on building a bomb shelter, but hadn't gotten around to it yet. Once it was established that the civilian did not have a bomb shelter, we asked a series of questions about the basement. This could get tricky, and occasionally the interview would be terminated. We called them premature ejections. It was not that the questions were personal, really, but that people were simply unaccustomed to having anyone, particularly a high school boy in a madras shirt, stand on their front steps and inquire about their basement.

Is it a full- or half-basement?

What are its dimensions?

Is the basement well-ventilated with windows?

Do you have any dry goods, canned goods, or water stored in your basement in the case of emergency?

Seldom—not more than eight or nine times—did I encounter anyone who had made any preparations such as storing food or water. When someone had made them, however, the questions then became more interesting.

How long ago did you first make such preparations?

How often do you change the water?

Does your bomb shelter have sources of artificial light?

Do you store blankets? Clothing? Medical supplies?

The few who had made preparations were always pleased to respond. They seemed proud, as though they were doing their duty, and some spoke with an assurance that suggested that they were destined to survive, no matter what the Ruskies threw at us. But some people, the premature ejections, became wary and simply shut the door. More than once it was suggested that I might be casing their house. One elderly man, standing on the wide porch of an old Victorian house, said, "Son, this is New England. We don't have basements. We have cellars."

II

There was nothing unusual about 647 Patton Road. Like all the houses in Forest Glen, it was a small two-story structure, a variation on the same basic design. After several days of canvassing, I could just look at the front of a house and guess its interior layout. This house had white clapboards with green trim, and in the front door were three small diamond-shaped windows arranged in a diagonal pattern. A faded sticker in the lower right-hand window said *Beware of Dog—No Solicitors.*

Kevin and I had debated how to deal with these stickers. We agreed that it was an invasion of privacy to knock, so we simply circled the address on our maps and moved on. But for some reason the dual warning—a dog *and* no solicitors—wouldn't allow me to just walk away. I opened the screen and knocked on the front door, figuring to give the residents their ten seconds. I half expected to hear a dog bark. Instead, the door was opened almost immediately. She was about my age, maybe a year or so older. I don't know how we determined these things, but in high school I could tell a sophomore from a junior from a senior from a college freshman with remarkable accuracy. Her light brown hair was wet, matted to her skull, and she was wearing a yellow bathrobe. There didn't seem to be a great deal behind the lapels, but there was a mole just below her collarbone that had the blush pink color of some nipples.

"Yes?" There was a peculiar echo to her voice.

I went into my spiel: "Hello, my name is Rick—"but then stopped, because my voice was echoing, too. Looking beyond her, I realized that there was no furniture in the living room (this one to the left, with an archway to the dining room at the back of the house).

She smiled, her lips matching that pink mole. "You're our first visitor," she said. Then she paused, and her expression changed, as though she recognized me. "Isn't it awful muggy out there?"

I nodded, then began scribbling the last name on the door plate.

"That's not us," she said. "We just moved in. Our name's Rosinsky."

I began erasing what I had written, and there was something about eraser crumbs on a humid afternoon that made me sorry I had knocked.

"Come in and do that," she said. "I just made some lemon-ade."

Our directives did not prohibit us from entering a dwelling. It was not encouraged, but occasionally a civilian, often an elderly woman, would invite me in, and usually a cold drink was of-fered. Kevin claimed to have had sex with several civilian women (none of them elderly), but the best one was the illegal alien with a Swedish accent.

And I knew what Kevin would say. *"Rosinksy?* Definitely a spy, Rick, a *red agent."*

As she led me into the kitchen (to the right off the dining room), she asked, "Don't you love that business about the Cynics, Epi-cureans and Stoics?"

•

Thursday afternoons Kevin and I parked downtown, lowered the radio to a respectable volume, and acted like we were just waiting for someone doing a quick errand. Kevin wore sunglasses for this; I put on my Red Sox cap. We called it The Drop.

On this particular afternoon, our contact, Mr. Ruckleshouse (or R, in code), arrived in a green Pontiac and parallel parked with just one hand.

"Jesus," Kevin whispered. "Every week, a masterpiece."

R got out of his sedan, looked up and down the sidewalk as he buttoned his suitcoat, then walked into Friendly's Ice Cream. His stride was slow, and his arms seemed too long for the rest of him. Once he was inside, we'd get out of the VW bug and follow him. He sat in a booth, and when we slid into the bench across from him he stared at us as though he'd never seen us before. He was somewhere between thirty and forty, smoked Lucky Strikes, and had a fat gold ring on his left pinky. His black hair was smoothed straight back, and it was so greased that it picked up the light in a way that reminded me of the grooves in a record album. "All right," he said, "show me what you got." We never took his air of disappointment seriously. Behind his flat gray eyes and deadpan delivery we knew he was saying *You don't fool me—I know what it's like to be high school guys like you. I know what's really on your minds.*

We laid our clipboards on the table. R removed our surveys, tallied them up, then slipped them into a manila envelope that bore the seal of the Commonwealth of Massachusetts.

"Why the slow day Tuesday?" he asked.

"Remember those thunderstorms all afternoon?" I said.

"So, nobody's home when it rains?"

"Wicked thunderbolts all around my car," Kevin pleaded. "The only thing that saved us was my tires."

"Wicked thunderbolts." R ordered Cokes for us, regular coffee for himself. He then removed the small leather notebook from inside his suitcoat and did some calculations with a mechanical pencil that probably had a microphone in it. We drained our Cokes and talked for a few minutes. About the Red Sox, who weren't going to win the pennant this year. About certain Friendly's waitresses. About anything but what we'd been doing all day. Through it all R was totally disinterested.

Finally he reached into his suitcoat once again, this time removing two small manila envelopes. He dropped them on the table; each had our last name written in pencil in the top right-hand corner. Then he slid out of the booth and as he walked away he said, "Gentlemen."

"I think he's a G-man washout," Kevin whispered. Handing me my envelope, he added, "And you're a capitalist *pig.*"

I punched him hard in the upper arm.

•

Two nights a week my summer was suspended for three hours. I drove my mother's Dodge Dart into Boston and attended a class at BU. It was a survey course in Greek and Roman Civilization, given in a lecture hall with brick walls and no windows. More than a hundred students attended and fortunately the room was air conditioned.

I thought I had checked out every girl in the hall, but somehow I had missed Melissa Rosinsky. Perhaps it was because she didn't wear her bathrobe to class. When we sat in her hot, nearly empty kitchen, drinking iced lemonade, we discussed our lecturer, Professor Laura Jacobs.

"She's really something, isn't she?" Melissa said.

"Yeah, she knows everything that's ever happened to the human race."

"So, you haven't noticed those legs? The tits?" I'd been in the house less than five minutes. She was still wet from a shower, and I was sweaty from pounding the streets of Forest Glen all day. I felt caught and she smiled. "I've never seen such a roomful of attentive men."

"It's like she gives off a scent," I said.

Melissa put both hands behind her head, raised her long straight hair off the back of her neck and held it on top of her skull. She had a slender neck and arched eyebrows that suggested both humor and curiosity. "What is this?" She nodded toward my clipboard on the table. "Magazine subscriptions? Or do you want me to register for the Republican Party?"

So I asked the preliminary questions and learned that she had recently moved here with her father, who had been transferred from Syracuse to Boston. He was an engineer for BLM, one of the tech firms out on Route 128.

When I asked about other family members, she hesitated. "My mother's still in New York." I looked up from my clipboard. Melissa was picking at a crust of dried food stuck to the table top. "I guess you can't put her down as a resident yet."

"When will she come?"

"I'm not sure." She was using her thumbnail expertly, prying and lifting what appeared to be a piece of hardened spaghetti from the wood. "The house in Syracuse needs to be sold. Most of our furniture's still there."

I left the line where I was going to write her mother's name blank.

"What exactly is this survey about? This isn't the census?"

"No. Are you ready?" I waited for her to look up from the crust of food. "Does this house have a bomb shelter?"

Something went out of her shoulders, some tension. She stood up and went to the sink. Gazing out the window into the back yard, she said, "Yes, I guess it does."

It was at least ninety degrees in that kitchen, but I suddenly had chills and goosebumps. "Holy shit. I've never had one before. This is my first bomb shelter."

"What's that mean?"

"I'll get to ask the questions on the left side of this form."

She came back to the table and picked up my clipboard. "Dimensions? Capacity? Water? Food supply?" I could feel the heat from her on my shoulder. Then, suddenly, she handed me the clipboard, went to the refrigerator, and got out the pitcher of lemonade. Light from the interior bulb passed through her yellow bathrobe and I could see the outline of her narrow hips. She refilled our glasses, sat across from me, and said, "I can't answer them accurately. I haven't even been in the bomb shelter. I'd show it to you, but it's locked and my father has the key." She sipped her lemonade, then laughed, soaring notes that echoed through the nearly empty house. "Imagine, if they dropped the big one right *now,* and we couldn't get in the shelter because it's *locked?"*

•

"*This* is giving me a wicked hard-on," Kevin yelled over the radio as we sped down Route 9. "You found a *bomb shelter!*" We'd been coming back to this for a several days. "But you didn't *see* it?"

"No."

"Because it's locked?"

"Yeah."

"Where is it?"

"Why?"

"I just wanna know!" I looked out the side window. "I'm not going to *do* anything, you know."

"I know."

"So where?"

"In Forest Glen."

"Great, that boils it down to several hundred addresses. What street? Eisenhower? Bradley?"

I tinkered with the radio, turning the dial until I got The Stones' " Nineteenth Nervous Breakdown," and I turned it way up.

"This gives me a hard-on!" Kevin screamed.

"What doesn't?"

"I don't know! I haven't found it yet!"

•

The Cynics, which translates literally to mean "the dogs," believed in the value of freeing oneself from desire. Their founder, Diogenes of Sinope (c. 412-323 B.C.), lived in a barrel, and he walked around Athens in the daytime carrying a lantern, looking for honest men. Upon meeting Alexander the Great in Corinth, he said to the king, "You're blocking my sun."

The Epicureans, founded by Epicurus of Samos (342-270 B.C.), believed that rather than fearing the gods and death, people should

pursue happiness. Their reputation for pleasure-seeking is unde-
served, according to Professor Jacobs, as they believed that happiness could only be gained through self-control and self-denial.

The name Stoics (Zenon of Cyprus, 335-263 B.C.) derives from
the Athenian phrase *Stoa poikile* or "painted porch," where the
group first met. They were convinced that the human passions
should be ruled by reason, discipline and a sense of duty, and that
life should be devoted to the pursuit of virtue.

When Professor Jacobs wrote on the chalkboard, something
remarkable happened to her calves; the muscles swelled and graceful ridges rolled beneath her skin. Her age wasn't easy to determine—something about women after a certain point that I didn't
understand. One night I overheard two other students, older
guys who must have been in college, speculating on her age as we
filed out of the lecture hall. One guy thought she wasn't quite
thirty; the other swore she had to be thirty-two—she was definitely thirty-two because it was a scientific fact that women reach
their sexual peak at thirty-two, and Professor Jacobs was clearly
there.

I was eighteen and I was at my sexual peak as I stood on the
sidewalk of Commonwealth Avenue at nine o'clock on a hot July
night, when a female hand tapped my right shoulder. There was
no question, it was a female hand, and my first fleeting thought
as I turned was that it was Professor Jacobs, who wanted me to
escort her to her car or, even better, to her apartment in the Back
Bay, where she would ask me to come up for a minute, which
would lead to something to drink—which would in turn lead to
something beyond my best eighteen-year-old erotic fantasies.
However, the female hand belonged to Melissa Rosinsky, and she
looked quite different. She wore an enormous blue sundress.
Her hair was tied up in a bun at the back of her head, and her
large-framed glasses had thick lenses which made her eyes huge.
She removed the glasses and said, "Boo!"

I offered her a ride home. She said she usually drove in herself,
except on nights like this when her father worked late, which
meant she had to take the bus into town. Driving out Route 9,

she asked me what year I was, meaning she assumed I was already in college. We were at a stoplight in Brookline, and I fidgeted with the radio buttons a moment. The Red Sox game was on, but I found some music and left it there. Then I told her I was a freshman—would be, anyway, in the fall. The light changed and I kept my eyes on the road, but I could feel her watching me. It seemed that in the silence some adjustment was taking place because she had thought I was older. Then she told me that she had been a freshman last year, which sounded odd (why not just say she was going to be a sophomore?), and that she would be a freshman again this coming year. She had gone to Cornell last fall, and she ran into trouble and left school in the middle of winter term. Then her father was transferred from Syracuse to the main office on Route 128. She had been admitted to Boston University on the condition that she take four credits in summer school so that she could raise her Grade Point Average.

We joked about GPAs: they were a symptom of the disease that afflicts adolescents. *Did you hear about Bobby? He came down with a low GPA. They say he's on probation for one semester and after that he's finished.* As we drove through Newton I told her about how I had been accepted to St. Mark's in Vermont on the condition that I go to summer school. Her silence at this suggested the obvious: why would a college with such a good reputation even accept someone with a low GPA?

"I play hockey," I said. "Nobody would take me with my grades, but several schools offered me a sports scholarship."

"Hockey—that's a very violent sport."

"Hockey's a physical game."

"It's one of those sports where the idea is to score goals."

"That's the point of most sports," I said, "to score runs, points, goals, whatever."

"It's always about scoring, and *goals,*" she whispered in disgust.

"But not for the goaltender. For us it's all about making saves."

"Jesus," she said, laughing, "now you wanna be a Christ figure?"

"No, I just want to pass this course. I don't get to lace up my skates again until I do."

When we pulled into her driveway, there were no lights on in the house. I shut off the ignition and we sat for a moment, listening to the ticking of the hot engine.

"What?" she said. I ran my fingers around the bumps on the steering wheel. "You want to ask me something. I can tell."

I wanted to ask her what kind of trouble she'd been in freshman year. But I said, "You told me the other day you'd get the key from your father. When should I come and see your bomb shelter?"

She watched her dark house and took a long time to answer. Her knees were lean and tanned. "I don't know. I haven't asked him about the key yet." There was uncertainty in her voice, which reminded me of when we had been sitting at her kitchen table and I was asking about how many members of the family were residents. "Listen," she said, "can I ask you something?"

"Sure."

"It's kind of a favor, but my father tends to work late a lot of nights, and I hate taking the bus into town—"

"Sure, I'll give you a lift into school."

III

At first Kevin just wore a bandana. Some kids started with the tie-dye T-shirts or the bellbottoms or the granny glasses. But by the Fourth of July he was wearing a red bandana and letting his hair grow.

Professor Jacobs had moved on to the Roman Empire, and on our trips in and out of Boston it seemed Melissa and I talked about everything. Since April both Bobby Kennedy and Martin Luther King, Jr., had been assassinated. This thing, this paranoia, seemed to be affecting everyone. Some nights in the lecture hall it was palpable. Professor Jacobs often drifted away from Nero (r. 54-68 A.D.) or Spartacus (d. 71 A.D.) and would start in on Lyndon Johnson and the war. Frequently her voice trembled, and the hall would become absolutely silent. Once she had to excuse herself and left the room.

The drinking age in the Commonwealth of Massachusetts was twenty-one, but I looked old enough to buy. I knew there were certain stores, one in Cleveland Circle, several in Cambridge, where they weren't too particular. I thought I knew the trick: if a kid goes in and just tries to buy beer, they kick him out; but if he goes in and buys beer and hard stuff, he won't get carded. I was buying a lot of beer and vodka, so much that we began to bury it in the woods off Algonquin Road. We'd go out into the woods and dig up a case and a bottle and get shitfaced. There were often five or six of us guys, all waiting to go away to different colleges in the fall.

One night Kevin showed up in the woods with a nickle bag. I refused to smoke dope because of hockey. I feared smoking grass would do something permanent to my head and affect my reflexes, which are essential to a goalie. I watched as they passed the pipe, inhaled and held it down. Not much seemed to happen. We talked about music a while, then some of the other guys drifted off into the woods. Finally I was sitting on a log in the dark with Kevin. He was talking about Hendrix and Cream, then he stopped in mid-sentence. We just listened to the woods, until I said, "You okay?"

"Yeah." His voice was small, nervous, a bit giddy. He took a deep breath and said with absolute sincerity, "Wow."

•

I couldn't stop wondering what kind of trouble Melissa had been in at Cornell. It must have had to do with drinking, drugs or sex—or all three. There was something about her I couldn't name, as though she'd done things and been places that were remarkably different, and that in going there and doing them she herself had been different, and now she was back, but not completely; there was something quiet and protective about her, and there was something of the survivor, too, as though she'd had some real scare, and since then she couldn't help but proceed with caution, as though at any moment she might lose control and the force of that earlier experience might haul her back to the brink. It was like I imagined people who had kicked addictions must live, always aware that the habit could again overwhelm them. Perhaps it was even a question of sanity. Maybe her trouble had led her to a nervous breakdown, and she was constantly aware of the possiblity that she could slip back into a state of helplessness. But what was sanity? Was she sane, or was she just acting sane? She was protecting something, hiding something, I was sure. Though we *seemed* to talk about everything, driving in and out of Boston, I was aware that she was avoiding certain things:

her trouble freshman year; her father who never seemed to be home; the lack of furniture in the house; her mother who was still, apparently, in Syracuse, trying to sell their old house. Instead, we talked endlessly about ancient history, Dylan, menstruation, acne, Vietnam. Regardless of the subject, the underlying theme was paranoia. History, she believed, whether it concerned city-states or American involvement in Southeast Asia, was all about war. Dylan's lyrics were all about social injustice that nothing, not Dylan, not Martin Luther King, not Bobby Kennedy, not mass demonstrations, draft card burnings or marches on the Pentagon could rectify. Cramps and pimples (she had a lot of the former, few of the latter) were about a body that was not in harmony with itself. When she talked her eyes got even larger behind her thick glasses, and there was an intensity that seemed to emanate from her like radiation—I couldn't see it, but I could feel it. It affected my nervous system, making me feel jumpy and sometimes even giddy. I worried that I was getting paranoid myself.

One night, driving out Route 9, we were talking about comic books. We both still loved the Spy vs. Spy cartoon in *Mad Magazine*. I said that when I was around thirteen I went through a period where I read all these comics that were about the aftermath of World War III. The scenarios were always similar. A handful of people manage to get underground just before the nuclear bombs hit; they survive for months, even years, then they finally emerge to find nothing but a world of urban rubble inhabited by vicious bands of mutants intent upon hoarding the remaining precious supplies necessary for survival—food, water, clothing, fuel. Somehow the underground people overcome all odds and the story ends with some glimmer of hope for the future of humanity. The survivors will work together to rebuild society, to govern themselves in a way that will ensure that such weapons of destruction will never be developed and deployed again, and of course they will reproduce, with the intention of teaching their offspring how to avoid the mistakes of the past.

When we pulled into her driveway, Melissa asked, "Do you

think that'll happen? That we're on the brink of some apocalypse?"

"I don't know. Even if we were, what could we do about it?"

She looked at me a moment, then did something that took me
by surprise. She slid across the red vinyl seat and hugged me. Up
until this we'd been nothing but platonic. It gave us the freedom
to talk the way we did, I thought, but now I could feel her smooth
bare arms around my neck. At first I attempted to make it a
friendly hug, brotherly and protective, but that soon changed as
her body fit tighter to mine. I could smell her hair and feel her
small breasts against my ribs. Then she kissed me, her mouth
open so that I could feel her tongue. Finally she drew away and
whispered, "Come in the house."

"Your father, won't he be home soon?"

"He's away on business."

She leaned back and looked at me through her glasses. I don't
know what she saw: fear, reluctance, eagerness, an eighteen-year-
old male recklessly at the peak of his sexuality; possibly all of
these. We got out of the car and she led me into the dark house.

IV

R simply watched as I drained my Coke. Kevin had gone to the men's room, and I was worried. Our week's survey sheets were spread out on the booth table. "What's going on?" R asked. I shrugged. "Come on, he's hardly covering half the territory you or any of the other surveyors cover."

"Really?"

R's gaze said *Don't mess with me, kid. Don't even think about it.*

"I don't know," I said, and worked on my Coke.

"He's on something." I stared at R again, certain that my eyes were confirming what he was saying. "He's high, isn't he? Stoned on something."

"I don't think so. It's just the way Kevin is—"

"You just have to look at him. That shirt. The bandana. Those stupid pants some of 'em are wearing now. When's the last time he had a haircut?"

Kevin came back to the booth, banging his knee as he slid in.

R put our pay envelopes on the table, staring at Kevin. "Next Monday, before you start, you meet me here."

Kevin leaned back. "Why?"

"Meet me here at eight-thirty." R started to slide out of the booth. "Clean yourself up between now and then, or you're through." He stood up and walked away. He didn't say "Gentlemen."

Kevin raised his arm, stuck his nose in his armpit and sniffed loudly. "What, I don't smell so bad, do I?"

"You always do." I slugged him in the other arm. Got him good, too.

•

Professor Jacobs was absent that night, so her teaching assistant ran a film about the fall of the Roman Empire. Corny stuff with senators in togas, gladiators, chariot races. It was a goof. There were snickers and laughter throughout the lecture hall, and someone had lit a joint. The feast and orgy scene that attempted to portray the decadence of Rome brought cheers and applause. Throughout the film I had my left hand down the front of Melissa's shorts. She tried to sit still, but after a while I could feel her shifting ever so slightly, adjusting the angle of her pelvis, and there was this tremor that seemed to run through her entire body.

As I drove out of Boston on Route 9 Melissa was stretched out on the red vinyl seat, her head above my lap. At stoplights I just kept looking straight ahead and toyed with the radio. Twice truckers honked as they passed.

When we got to her house we went inside and never even bothered turning on the lights. It was a Thursday night; her father was on business in San Francisco; my parents had gone down to the Cape with my brother and sister for the weekend. There was no reason for me to go home. Sometime around midnight, I pulled on my shorts, went out and put the car in the garage.

Part of this had to do with the fact that it would be over soon. It was nearly August, and in a month I'd be packing off to school in Vermont and Melissa would be attending BU full-time. For some reason that made the nature of our commitment to what we were doing to each other more genuine, more immediate. We hadn't talked about what we would do in the fall, whether we'd continue to see each other; we hadn't talked about anything like love. It felt like we were a couple of kids getting away with something. And it felt good.

In the early morning light we were lying naked on her bed—a single bed in a room that only had a bureau and a stereo on the floor. No photographs, no pictures on the walls.

"It's Friday," she said. "You could skip work."

"I'd like to but R is getting pissed off. He's on to Kevin."

"Know what I'd really like?"

"Hm?"

"You to stay the weekend."

I stared at the ceiling a moment. I explained that I was supposed to drive down to the Cape after work and join my family. "I suppose I could call them and tell them I'm staying up here for the weekend. Besides, the traffic to the Cape Friday nights is unbelieveable."

She rolled over on top of me, and her hair fell down so that our faces were inside this veil of fine dark silk. "I'm so blind," she whispered, "but I'm close enough to see you."

"And what do you see?"

"I can see for miles." We laughed. Then, as she lowered her face to mine, she sang, "I can see for miles and miles and miles and miles."

•

Kevin was sitting on my back steps when I pulled my mother's car up to the curb around eight-thirty. "You're late," he said. "You drive today." He picked up his clipboard and walked down the driveway. It was a short, noisy journey. His sandals slapped against his bare heels, his wide-wale corduroy bellbottoms made a whooshing sound with each stride, and his love beads clicked against his tie-dye T-shirt. He was wearing sunglasses with purple lenses, and a woman's wide-brimmed hat—bright yellow—with a long orange feather tucked in the band.

"Hurry up," I said, "before the neighbors call the police."

He was stoned already and simply getting into the car was an ordeal. Leaning toward me, he said in a small, creepy voice, "Rick was out all night. Somebody's getting laid."

I pushed the drive button and floored the accelerator. Dodge Darts were extraordinary for their push-button transmission, not their engines. We didn't peel out, we didn't leave rubber. We drove to the section of town called The Falls and parked across from the old mill on the Charles River. I reached into the back seat to get my clipboard and I.D., when I realized Kevin had an envelope in his hand. Tilting the open mouth of the envelope, something small and glossy fell into his palm. It looked like a fishscale.

"The hell is that?"

"Windowpane."

"Windowpane?"

"LSD. You put it in your eyes."

"Jesus, Kevin."

"This is my last day looking for bomb shelters, man. I'm not cutting my hair for Lyndon Johnson, for the Domino Theory, or for R, even if he *can* parallel park one-handed." He carefully put the windowpane back into the envelope, which he folded up. "When we finish this afternoon, I'm gonna do like Jimi Hendrix says and wave my freak flag high. Man, I'm gonna *see the light at the end of the tunnel!*"

V

After canvassing The Falls all day, I met Kevin as planned back in the park across the river from the old mill. He was lying in the grass, singing Cream's "White Room" at the top of his lungs.

"You took that windowpane stuff," I said.

"In the white room, with black curtains, at the station!" He strummed his belly and did a decent verbal imitation of Eric Clapton's wah-wah pedal.

It took me about twenty minutes to get him out of the park. First he tried to crawl, saying something about being an earthworm, and he had to watch out for hungry birds; then for some reason he needed to lick the bark of a maple tree. Finally I got him in the car. He couldn't go home like this, so I went to a payphone, called his house and explained to his kid brother that he was spending the night with me. Then I took him back to Forest Glen.

One look at Kevin and Melissa asked me, "What's this, your alter ego?" Kevin put his arms around her like he hadn't seen her in years.

We started in on her father's beer and whisky. She smoked joints with Kevin, and finally I said I'd try it. We were sitting on her bedroom floor in front of the stereo and we passed the joint around, and after about a half an hour I said nothing was happening. I didn't know what to expect. Strange colors? Some dream state? But there was nothing to it apparently. Until I realized that I had been staring hard at one of the small KLH speakers. We were listening to Cream's *Wheels Of Fire,* and when "Crossroads" came on, I couldn't get over the lead guitar.

Melissa leaned into my vision and said, "Hello?"

"That speaker. It's like the guitar is right *in* there. It's a very small guitar."

She laughed. "Welcome."

"Eric Clapton," Kevin said. "He's *God!*"

We listened to "Crossroads" over and over. After a while the three of us were lying on our backs on the floor, our heads right in front of the speaker with the lead guitar. Kevin's hands floated in the air above his face, turning and drifting to the music.

After listening to the song at least ten times, Melissa stood up and said, "I have a surprise for you." Lifting the bottom of her T-shirt, she dug into the coin pocket of her cutoffs and pulled out a key. "I found the extra in Dad's bureau today."

"Key to what?" Kevin asked.

"The bomb shelter," I said.

His head turned toward me on the hardwood floor. He was still wearing his purple sunglasses. He mouthed the words *bomb shelter?*

•

Getting downstairs to the basement was not just an ordeal, it was a trial. Not all the lights worked, so we had to find a flashlight. The batteries were dead, so we had to find candles. And matches. Then Melissa had to find her sneakers. Then Kevin had to go to the bathroom, which seemed to take forever.

Finally, we were descending the stairs to the basement. There was one dim light above the washer and dryer, but the far end of the basement was dark. We lit our candles and walked slowly. Kevin kept making sounds with his mouth—*oohs* and *ahhs*—and overhead we could hear Ginger Baker's long drum solo on "Toad" coming through the floor joists.

We reached a three-foot square metal door in the concrete wall.

Melissa unfastened the padlock and yanked the door open. Bending over, we held our candles in the opening of a low round tunnel made of galvanized steel.

"Well?" she said.

I went first, crawling and holding the candle ahead of me; it was only about five yards, but it seemed to take forever. Then I stepped out into the bomb shelter, which was just high enough for me to stand upright. It was no more than ten feet long and eight feet wide. There were shelves along one wall, stocked with canned goods, bottles of water, blankets—everything was neatly stacked and organized. On the opposite wall was a bunk bed constructed with two-by-fours and plywood. The three of us sat on the lower bunk. Our candles illuminated the shelter quite well. The air was cool, with little humidity, which was a relief.

We sat there for a long time, looking around, until Kevin got up and counted the rolls of toilet paper. He looked spooked, and periodically he would take a long deep breath and let it out loudly. Then he took his candle and began crawling back out the tunnel. I started after him, but Melissa grabbed my arm and led me back to the bed. "Kevin," she said, her voice echoing down the tunnel, "bring back some beer."

"And my clipboard," I called. "We'll do one last survey for R."

"Oh, man, the *survey.*" Kevin shut the door to the basement.

"And don't forget to come *back!*" I shouted. Sound in the confined space was interesting. Everything had a faint ring to it, as though we were in a cave.

"Welcome to the apocalypse," Melissa said as she leaned forward to kiss me. We lay down on the bed and got involved in a half-hearted, playful way. "How long do you think we could stand it down here?" she asked. "I mean if we really had to use it, if this was our only chance."

"That depends," I said, pulling up her T-shirt. Her nipple swelled in my mouth. I was desperate to no longer be a virgin; I suspected that Melissa was desperately trying to be one again. We'd found a fine compromise as we kissed and licked and sucked at each other's flesh, our breathing and groaning reverberating in the near dark.

•

I don't know how long I slept, a few minutes perhaps, long enough for our loins to cool but not dry. Melissa was still asleep. I got up, found a blanket on the shelf, and put it over her. The air was musty and one of our candles had gone out. Something didn't seem right. I thought it might be the dope wearing off, or perhaps the beer and whisky wearing off, or maybe it had to do with sex. Whatever, Melissa opened her eyes and I believe she saw it on my face.

"Try the door," she said.

I relit my candle from hers and crawled back out the tunnel. The door was locked. I pounded on the metal with my fist and shouted Kevin's name. Periodically I would pause to listen, but I could hear nothing beyond the door. When I returned to the shelter, Melissa was sitting up with the blanket around her. I got another blanket from the shelf and sat next to her. The wool was scratchy, but its weight was a comfort.

"The key," I said.

"I left it in the padlock."

"Well, that's something."

After a while, we lay together on the cot, wrapped in both blankets. We hugged each other for warmth. Periodically one of the candles would go out, and I would relight it with the other one. Later—several hours later—I got up and took stock of what was on those shelves. There were plenty of candles, and there was a two-burner propane stove for heating canned food. In the corner was a small air vent, connected to a pipe that went up into the ceiling. "This shelter would do well on the survey," I said. "We might last weeks in here without turning into total mutants."

"That's encouraging."

"It's interesting what they don't have," I said, lying down on the lower bunk again. "No books, no magazines, nothing to read except for what's on the labels of canned goods. Why didn't they plan for that?"

"What do you want, color TV?"

"No, but a radio would be a good idea."

She turned and faced the wall, curling up in a fetal position. "Maybe they planned on having stimulating conversations. And frequent sex."

I was beginning to see that that wasn't the case at all. "That goddamned survey," I said, turning so my back was to hers. "It misses the whole point."

•

When I awoke Melissa was cooking Dinty Moore beef stew. She had found a green flannel shirt and a pair of khaki army pants with big square pockets. They were too long so she wore them with the cuffs rolled up several times. She had laid out similar clothes on the bed. I got dressed and we ate out of the pot with spoons.

I can only describe the next few hours as domestic. We gave each other as much room as possible. To use the chemical toilet. To wash with bottled water. To be by ourselves. We were settling in for the long haul, and it was Melissa who established a sense of routine. There was no clock in the bomb shelter, so we had no idea how long we'd been down there. There was no sense of night or day. I thought that it must be dawn by then, but there was no way to be certain.

"He must have really tripped out," she said. We were lying on our backs in the bunk—she was in the lower; I was in the upper, at her request. "But eventually that shit he's taken has to wear off."

"Knowing Kevin, he's simply forgotten we're down here and he's wandered off. It's quite possible that he had more of that windowpane, and he's somewhere still blasted out of his mind. I hope he's having a good time, because when we get out of here I'm going to kill him."

"No, it's not his fault."

"What are you *talking* about?"

"Please, don't raise your voice, Rick. I can hear you. It's our fault. Any society that even thinks it needs a bomb shelter deserves to use it."

"Which is that? The view of the Cynics, the Epicureans, or the Stoics?"

"That's a good question," she said. "I wish Professor Jacobs were here so we could examine it carefully."

I sat up in my bunk quickly, and banged my head against the ceiling. *"Christ."*

"Are you all right?"

"I think I'm bleeding."

She climbed into the upper bunk and examined my scalp. "No blood," she said. "But you've got a good welt there."

"What happened last year?" I demanded. "What kind of trouble did you have at Cornell?" Her hands had been parting my short hair, but now she dropped them in her lap and turned her head away. "Booze, drugs, sex, right?"

"A little of the first two," she said, "and I ended up having an abortion."

"Was it love or was it some frat party?"

"I wish it had been love."

"Love," I said. "Is that what this is, love?"

"I don't know, do you?"

"I'm no frat boy."

"You're the first boy I've been with since. Have you ever been in love?"

"I suppose."

"What happened?"

"She fell in love with someone else," I said. "Do we have to have all these questions?"

"Does it matter whether we're in love down here?"

"Kevin!" I shouted, rapping my fists on the ceiling. "Where *are* you!"

"Rick, Rick, please. No point in getting excited."

"What's happening to you? You're accepting this? It's like you want to be locked in."

"I'm accepting that it's necessary."

"Melissa, there aren't any nuclear bombs falling in your backyard."

"It doesn't matter. There *could* be, so we need to know if this means of survival works." There was a tranquility to her voice that was frightening. She put her arms around me and kissed the welt on my skull. "Don't you see? The apocalypse is here."

"Let me *out,*" I said. I rolled over her and jumped down from the upper bunk. For a long time I paced back and forth. Three strides, turn; three strides, turn.

In a soft, inspired voice, Melissa began to sing "Will the circle be unbroken—"

"Don't!" I shook the frame of the bunk. "Don't even *think* of singing that song!"

"You're a very violent person, even for a hockey player."

"I'm very physical."

"That's why my father left my mother in Syracuse," she said. "She was very physical. She was physical with our neighbor, Mr. Linhardt. She was physical with Dr. Kerry, who removed my tonsils. She was physical with a man named Walter who used to call the house in the middle of the night."

"I'm sorry, really. But your parents splitting up is not the apocalypse."

She stared at me with absolute pity in her eyes, then turned to the wall. Suddenly I felt exhausted. I climbed in the lower bunk and passed out.

•

I was awakened by a tremendous clap of lightning, followed seconds later by the rumble of thunder. I could hear pounding overhead, and it took a moment to realize that it was a hard rain falling in the backyard. Then I realized that Melissa was lying next to me, shivering. I put my arms around her. She buried her face against my chest and she cried loudly, her body wracked by deep sobs and shudders. She cried for a long time while overhead the thunder and lightning grew more violent, and the rain drummed on the earth. "At the moment," I whispered in her ear, "this isn't such a bad place to be." She held me tightly and her sobs began to subside. As the thunder began to move off, we drifted into sleep again.

•

We were mopping up a small puddle of rain water that had dripped from the air vent. Bad sign: leaky bombshelters wouldn't have a chance against radiation.

"Do you think you have a future?" she asked.

"That depends on my GPA."

"Let's assume it's good, what do you do?"

"I don't know." I wrung the wet towel out in the pot. "I just graduated from high school. I don't have a clear plan like some kids who are going to be lawyers by the time they're twenty-six, then run for office. This town's full of those kids. Why do you think I hang out with a bozo like Kevin?"

"I like Kevin," she said.

"I do too. But he can be forgetful."

"A GPA means nothing," she said.

"Amen."

"This is it right here: food, clothing and shelter."

"I was hoping for something with a better view."

"Say that door opens right now."

"You wish."

"We walk out into the sun, holding hands," she said, "like those comic book characters who defeat the nuclear mutants and are going to give humanity another chance."

"You're a romantic."

"Know what you're going to spend your life building?"

I was draping the wet towel from the shelf and weighing it at the top corners with canned goods. "This," I said. "I'm going to build my bomb shelter."

She nodded, then reached up and began unbuttoning her flannel shirt.

VI

There was a light at the end of the tunnel. Melissa and I lay in each other's arms, and we squinted toward the flashlight beam.

"You all right?" Kevin asked, his voice echoing down the tunnel.

We got out of the bunk. We were both naked. Kevin's light went over Melissa pretty thoroughly. "Shut that thing off," I said.

"Listen, I don't know what *happened.* I—I got all screwed up, man. Must have passed out. You been down here all *night,* and when I woke it was like afternoon. At first I couldn't even remember where I was or that you were *down* here. Then it started to come back to me—geez, I'm really sorry. I suppose you're going to *really* slug me in the arm, but I just like completely lost it and—"

"Kevin, just shut up."

"Okay."

Melissa took hold of my hand. "Now, shut the door, Kevin."

"What?"

"You heard her," I said.

"Don't lock it," she said. "Just close it, and we'll come out when we're ready."

After a moment, Kevin pushed the door shut.

We got dressed and sat together on the lower bunk. Melissa had found a deck of cards among the toiletries, and for a long time we played hearts and blackjack.

"See," I said, "no apocalypse out there. It's just Kevin."

"You don't suppose he's radioactive."

"Naa. Born mutant. Product of a nuclear American family. Doesn't need no Commie A-bombs to mess up his genes."

"Knew I liked him."

The bomb shelter felt different then, because we remained by choice. It was not a matter of how long before we could get out; it was how long could we stay. The lesser of two concerns, certainly, but one which we thought we'd earned.

"If we go out there," she said, just as she laid down her cards, beating me again at hearts, "and the air raid sirens were to go off, we can always come back here."

"I suppose," I said, gathering up the cards. "But it would mean we'd always have to live within minutes of this house. You plan on doing that?"

She looked horrified. "A life in Forest Glen? *No.*"

"Well then. What's the point—what are the odds of survival? And what is survival under those circumstances? You keep yourself tied to one place on earth where you think you might have the slightest chance."

"Shackled," she said, taking the cards and shuffling. "The word is shackled."

"Fine. I'd rather go out there and live, knowing that at any moment the sirens could go off."

"In spite of the impending apocalypse?"

"Yes. Why get so hellbent on survival you forget to live?"

"Cynic? Epicurean? Stoic? Where's Professor Jacobs when we need her?"

"Out there, somewhere."

We were hungry again, so we looked through the canned goods and chose Chef Boyardee Ravioli. After heating up two cans, we stood at the stove, eating out of the pot with one spoon. We ate slowly, feeding each other and nothing, I mean *nothing,* ever tasted better.

VII

Monday morning I was sitting alone in a booth at Friendly's when R came in. "Where's our love child?" he asked.

I waited until he sat down, then I pushed Kevin's clipboard and badge across the table. "He decided not to get a haircut."

R glanced up at the waitress and said, "Coffee, regular." When she left, he whispered, "Too many goddamned kids going to college, that's the problem."

The man was a mutant. I picked up my clipboard from beside me on the bench and laid it on the table. The man was the worst kind of mutant because with the hair and the suit and the nicotine-stained fingers and teeth he blended in so well.

"Christ," he said. "You going to grow your hair and wear beads, too?"

"No. I just can't knock on any more doors. It's nobody's business who's got a bomb shelter anyway." He glanced down at my clipboard, his expression becoming focused, curious, perhaps even excited. "It's no joke," I said. "I found one. That's why I'm quitting. It was terrific, R. You could survive in it a long time. Well, maybe you couldn't. But with the right company, I might even be able to live in it."

"The address isn't complete—just Forest Glen."

"It's a start."

"It's not valid without a full address."

I got out of the booth. I was still wearing my badge because when I went to Friendly's I wasn't sure what I was going to do. After all, it was a job. But I also imagined that if I did quit, it would be more dramatic to take the badge off in R's presence and drop it on the table—a moment right out of the old Western movies. But I didn't even take the badge off. Fact was, I felt I'd earned the right to keep it. So it was better than a Western, because when R looked at the badge, I said, "You want this, you're going to have to take it off me." Then I turned and walked out the door.

•

We took our final exam in Professor Jacobs' survey of Greek and Roman Civilization. Melissa and I had crammed together, and though I didn't have all the dates down cold I knew halfway through the multiple choice questions that I'd bring up my GPA enough to satisfy St. Mark's. The essay question felt real good. I discussed how the popular belief that the Roman Empire had been militarily defeated by invading barbarians was erroneous; that, in fact, over the course of centuries it was barbarian assimilation, first into Roman military, then political and social life, that eventually resulted in there no longer being any true Roman Empire. Professor Jacobs, her handwriting as graceful as her calves, said that my essay was thoughtful and idealistic, particularly the passage about how an advanced civilization seeking virtue was the very essense of human survival.

Melissa and I spent a lot of time together the rest of the summer. We pretended to spot mutants everywhere. At Hawthorne Lake where we went swimming. At a Boston Pops concert at the Hatch Shell on the Charles. But at Fenway Park we didn't see one mutant—only fans, disappointed that the Red Sox weren't going to win the pennant again that year. Kevin was often along for the ride, and he pretty much stuck to beer. He was a bit perturbed by the fact that we were talking about mutants and laughing, and he didn't get it. Then we filled him in and he started seeing mutants everywhere. Still, he wasn't used to the idea of not being the one who made the jokes. I still slugged him in the arm now and then.

I finally met Mr. Rosinsky. He was one of these quiet, balding fathers who seemed perpetually overworked and tired. I liked him. He drove up to Syracuse one weekend in late August, and it appeared that he and his wife were going to try once more. Melissa was pleased about that, particularly because it meant that she'd be able to live in a dorm at BU.

Then we all went off to college (boys who didn't heard from the draft board). Melissa and I kept up for a while. Phone calls, letters, and I hitched a ride down to Boston a couple of times during the fall. But once winter set in I only got out of Vermont when the hockey team traveled by bus to another school. We lost touch, but we didn't forget each other. We had our own lives to lead.

Cold

Liesl Tiomenen saw the man from her kitchen window. The snow was so heavy he was hardly visible at the edge of the woods. He stared toward the house, his arms folded so his hands were clamped under his armpits. He wore a soiled canvas coat and blue trousers, but no hat. His stillness reminded her of the deer that often came into the yard to eat the carrots and apples she left for them.

Liesl went out into the attached shed and took Harold's .30-.30 Winchester down off the rack, then opened the back door, holding the rifle across her chest. The man didn't move. The north wind chilled the right side of her face; her fingers on the stock felt brittle. He was young, not more than twenty-five, and she could see that he was shivering.

"All right," she said. "You can come inside."

He began walking immediately, his legs lifting up out of the snow that was almost to his knees.

"Slowly," she said. "And put your hands down at your sides where I can see them."

He stopped and watched her. Then he lowered his arms to his sides and continued on toward the house.

•

When the door opened, he had expected an old man or woman. Something about the house suggested that retired people lived there, the way it looked simple but well maintained. There were recent asphalt shingle patches on the roof, the windows had been freshly painted, and firewood was stacked against the shed. It was the smell of wood smoke that had drawn him toward the house.

But it was a woman, maybe in her early forties. She was tall and her long blond hair was tied in a thick braid which hung over her left shoulder. Her hands were large, and one thumb appeared to be smeared with mud. When he reached her, she pointed the rifle at his chest and he stopped. She stared at him a moment, her blue eyes showing neither panic nor fear, only determination. He tried to quit shaking, but it only made it seem worse.

"Okay," she said, stepping back into the shed. This close he could see that there was something odd about her mouth; her lips seemed out of kilter. When she spoke there was a kind of sag to the right side of her face, as though the muscles were lax. "Kitchen's that way."

He stepped into the shed and opened the door to the warm, heavy air of the house. There was the smell of burning wood, and something else that he couldn't identify—a pleasant scent of damp earth. It made him lightheaded, and his shaking only got worse.

•

He fell to the floor, his palms slapping the wood.

Liesl walked around him, watching his face. There was a small cut beneath his eye and twigs and pine needles were entangled in his short black hair. She poked him in the shoulder with the rifle, but he didn't respond. He wasn't faking. She went to the stove and turned on the burner beneath the teakettle. Reaching into the pocket of her flannel shirt, she took out a pack of cigarettes. She held the tip to the flame for a moment, then raised the cigarette to her lips and inhaled.

•

When he opened his eyes, she was standing at the stove, smoking a cigarette, the rifle tucked beneath one arm and angled down. Not exactly pointed at him, but not far off either.

"Can you get up?"

"I think so."

"Then sit in the chair by the radiator and keep your hands on the table."

He watched her raise the cigarette to that mouth, then the tobacco glowed. He inhaled through his nose and the smoke helped revive him. For a moment she looked pleased, then she reached into the pocket of her flannel shirt, took out a pack of Winstons and tossed them on the kitchen table.

"Thanks," he said. There was a book of matches beneath the cellophane. His hands were shaking so badly the first match waved out; the second he had a hard time holding steady to light the cigarette. When he got it lit, he watched the match flame burn down to his fingertips. After it went out, he said, "Nothing. Can't feel a thing."

"Rub them," she said. "Rub them together."

He did, working the palms slowly against each other.

"When'd you break out?"

"Two days ago. Musta walked fifty miles."

She smiled crookedly around her cigarette. "You're not twelve miles from the prison."

"The woods, they never stop up here."

"Why do you think they put prisons in the Upper Peninsula? You think you're the first one to try to walk away? They usually turn themselves in—you're lucky you haven't already frozen to death."

The teakettle whistled and he nearly jumped up from his seat.

She did everything with one hand, hardly taking her eyes off him. When she placed the mug of tea on the table, she said, "Have you eaten anything?"

"No."

"You drink that. I'll feed you, but first I got to be able to put this thing down."

"I won't do nothing."

"If you had done nothing, you wouldn't be in that prison." She opened the shed door, reached around the jamb and took something that rattled off a hook. It was a chain, the kind used for towing, coiled up like rope. She unlocked and removed the padlock, then put the chain on the kitchen floor by his feet. "Now, you wrap that around your middle a couple times, then run it round that radiator foot." Putting the padlock on the table, she said, "Then lock it."

He chained himself to the radiator, then picked up the mug. The heat from the tea stung his fingers.

•

She leaned the rifle in the corner by the stove and began to make him some eggs. Three scrambled eggs, with dark rye toast. When she wasn't watching him she listened to him; he was quiet and he hardly moved. When he finished drinking one mug of tea, she made him another.

She sat down across the table and watched him eat. There were acne scars on his neck, and his nose reminded her of boxers who have had the cartilage removed. She was surprised that he ate so slowly, that he didn't just eat like a dog. But he seemed to have trouble swallowing.

"Been so long since I ate," he said, when he was halfway through the eggs, "my stomach hurts. But they're good. They just go down hard." He glanced out the window frequently, toward the driveway, and she could see when it registered in his eyes. He tried to conceal it, but the next time he looked at her he was shy, like a child with a secret.

As she lit another cigarette she looked out at the snow where the drive was—the banks were over six feet high, and there was at least two feet of new snow in the drive. "My plowman came night before last," she said, "but it's been coming down so fast he can't get up the hill now. It's been like this all winter."

"Last year after we set the record for snow," he said, pushing away his empty plate, "we all thought this year couldn't be so bad."

"It's worse," she said. "We're more than four feet ahead of last year. At this pace they say we might get three-hundred inches."

One corner of his lips tucked in, creating a dimple. "My friend Bing's right. Says all people do outside is talk about the weather." He picked up the pack of cigarettes and tapped one out. "You can't get out of here and the police can't get in. How you going to get me back?"

"That's what you want, right?"

"I stay out there any longer, I'm dead." He touched the cut beneath his eye a moment. "I know what you're saying. Guys inside tell you about other escapees, how they walk away, then give themselves up because of the woods and the weather. I didn't believe them."

"You're not from the U.P."

"No, I'm from downstate. Always heard about winters up here, but you just don't believe it. You think they got to be lying. But they weren't, I know that now."

She went to the sink, soaked a washcloth, and gave it to him. "You better clean that cut."

He daubed at his face and winced, only smearing dirt. "It's fine."

"Right." She came around the table and took the washcloth from him. "Hold still." She put one hand on the back of his head and cleaned the cut. He stared up at her and didn't move, though when she touched the wound she could feel the muscles in his neck tighten as he tried to pull his head back against her hand. "How'd you do this?"

"Saw some coyotes on a ridge. Maybe they were wolves? I don't know. But they weren't no dogs. Then I tripped over a downed tree under the snow."

When she was finished she looked at the wound a moment before letting go of his skull. His clothes smelled bad and his hair was wet and dirty. "Where'd you think you were going?" she said as she went back to the sink to rinse out the washcloth.

"Dunno. Into Marquette and steal a car. I thought the snow

would keep them from finding me. Got lost instead."

"Yes, you did." She turned and leaned against the sink, drying her hands on a towel. He smoked and gazed out at the snow. "You been in long?"

"Two years, seven months, three days."

"Why?"

He drew on his cigarette, then crushed it out on his plate. "Had a girlfriend in Lansing. Say I raped and beat her."

"Did you?"

"Sort of."

"How long you in for?"

"Eight. She went blind in one eye, I guess. Now, when I go back, I don't know what I'll get." He turned his head from the window. "What happened to you?"

"Car accident. My husband and daughter were killed."

"I'm sorry."

"Are you?"

"Yes, I am."

She went to the phone on the wall and picked up the receiver. There was no dial tone. She hung up.

He was watching her. "Dead?"

"I'll try again in a while."

He leaned back in the chair and the chains rattled. "So you live way out here alone?"

"Harold and I built this house together, when we were your age. It was about all I had afterwards."

He glanced toward the door to the living room. "There's a smell—it's not the smoke, but something else."

She noticed that a puddle of water had formed around his boots. She picked up the rifle, then put the padlock key on the table. "Come in here and take those wet things off."

He unlocked himself and put the key next to the plate; then he coiled the chain up, gathered it against his stomach, and led her into the living room, which opened on to a large studio with skylights. He looked at the shelves of pottery, the wheel, the work benches, the kiln. "You can smell it way out there in the woods." He bent over and began unlacing his boots. "What if that phone doesn't come back?"

"We can always walk down to the store on the county road."

"How far is it?"

"A ways."

"Walk?"

"You ever wear snowshoes?"

"No."

"We could ski out, if you'd rather."

"The snowshoes'll be fine."

She stepped into the bedroom to get him some wool socks. When she looked up at the bureau mirror she saw that he was asleep on the couch, cradling the chains on his stomach.

•

When he awoke he lay beneath a gray blanket on the couch, with his feet sticking out the other end; she had put wool socks on him while he slept. "I thought I'd never feel my feet again."

She was sitting across the living room, the rifle resting against the arm of the stuffed chair. "You stayed out there much longer and you wouldn't have."

"I tried not to think about the cold, but it's all you think about. Same as being inside, really."

"What do you think about inside?"

He gazed at the ceiling a long time, then he smiled. "I know what most of the guys would say."

"I do too."

He turned his head on the armrest of the couch. She had put on a green sweater which made her breasts seem full. He couldn't take his eyes off them. When he looked at her face she was watching him with an even stare. He realized she was accustomed to men staring at her that way, that it was something she had endured for a long time. It appeared to bore her.

"Bing, he reads a lot and he tells me stuff. Says he has a theory: if you think about how some people have it worse, you won't find your situation so bad."

"Not a bad theory," she said. "What's he read?"

"All sorts of stuff. Lot of history. Tells me about battles and conquerors. Lately we've been into tortures. Bing found a whole book just on torture techniques. The Inquisition, Ivan The Terrible, Vlad The Impaler."

"Wasn't he the one Dracula's based on?"

"That's right," he said, staring at the ceiling again. "As a boy he had been a hostage of some sultan in Constantinople and he was buggered a lot. So later, when he's this fierce military leader, he scared the hell out of his enemies by impaling his prisoners. He used a long, thin needle—greases it, then shoves it up their ass until it comes out their mouth. Did it in a way that it would take days to die. He'd do thousands of people at a time, and plant them around his camp. Thousands on a skewer."

She was staring very hard at him, and her cheeks seemed flushed. "And Bing thinks it takes your mind off prison?"

"Yeah, but it only works for a while. You actually have to concentrate on that sort of thing and it gets old. Out there in the woods, it didn't work at all. I tried to think of everything, believe me, but I was just too cold."

"So much for theories."

He couldn't tell by her voice whether she was making a joke or being serious. When he looked at her he couldn't tell either; her eyes were just as steady as when she'd first opened the shed door.

"When you came outside with the rifle and pointed it at me, what would you have done if I had, you know, tried something?"

"What would you have tried?"

"Take the gun away."

She turned her head and stared into her pottery studio. "Suppose you had gotten the gun from me, what would you do?"

"Unload it."

She continued to gaze at her shelves of pots, so long that he began to wonder if she'd heard him. "Well, you didn't, and I didn't, and it stays loaded." She looked back at him. "Don't lose sight of that fact."

"I'm not dangerous or anything."

"Not now you aren't."

They didn't talk for a while. He stared at the ceiling and walls. What he had thought were shadows he realized was smoke residue from the kiln. The plaster had faint smudges built up around the slightest raised edge, whether it was a small imperfection in the wall, along the edge of moulding, or around a light switch plate. It gave flat surfaces relief as though someone had taken a pencil and shaded everything, first using the side of the lead point, then smearing the gray with a moist fingertip. On the wall by the door to the bedroom he noticed a small rectangle of white where a photograph had hung. His eyesight was good and he could even see the small black hole where the nail had been driven into the wall. It was like her life here: a white rectangle surrounded by not so white, two shades so close you don't notice the difference right away.

"You try the phone again?" he asked.

"Twice while you were asleep," she said. "Still out."

"What are we going to do?"

"You feel like you could walk out there again?" she asked. "This time properly dressed and with snowshoes."

"I'm not in any hurry to get back."

"I suppose you're not."

"It's nice here. Warm. I see why you stayed after—I see why you live here."

"We have to go soon if we're to get out before dark."

•

She gave him some of Harold's clothes: longjohns, a second pair of socks, a flannel shirt, a heavy sweater, good insulated boots, gloves, parka, a wool hat that could be pulled down over the ears. She let him change in the bathroom, telling him if he wanted to try and squeeze out the window he'd only get stuck in the drift on the north side of the house.

When they were both dressed they went out to the shed and

buckled on the snowshoes. Then they went outside and began walking south down the drive, which was a wide snowbound path through the woods. He led and she followed with the rifle. He walked slowly, with his head down, concentrating on each step.

"It's kind of a waddle," he said over his shoulder. It was hard to hear him because the wind was at their backs. "I feel like a baby in diapers." There was some joy in his voice, something she imagined he'd expressed seldom since going to prison.

"You're doing fine," she said.

"How far is 'a ways'?"

"We should get to the store at the crossroads before dark, if we take a shortcut over that hill."

He looked to his left. "It's steep."

"It's that or walk five miles around it."

•

His snowshoes were old, the varnished wood frame worn and splintered, and the mesh broken and mended in several places with dirty white shoelaces. The snowshoes didn't hold him up on top of the snow like he expected, but allowed him to sink down in the powder a good half foot; then he could feel the snow compress and support him. It was hard work, deliberately lifting his leg up and out of the snow with each step, and soon his groin muscles ached. By the time they were at the bottom of the drive, he had broken a sweat beneath the layers of her dead husband's warm clothes.

The road hadn't been plowed either and they walked down the middle of it, toward the hill. They were now walking east and the wind and snow struck them from the left. She walked to his right and a full stride behind, carrying the rifle across her chest. The wind was so steady that the snow was horizontal.

"You mind if I ask your name?" he asked.

"Liesl."

"Norman. How long ago was your accident?"

"Five years ago next April. It was during a spring blizzard."

"What did Harold do?"

"Lot of things. Carpentered. Drove heavy equipment. Hunted and fished for much of our food. There's a freezer locker in the shed that used to be stocked with venison, smoked whitefish, and coho salmon all winter."

"You're one of those live-off-the-land people I hear about up here. He hunted and you did pottery."

"Something wrong with that, Norman?"

"No. Seems like a lot of work though. I mean you can walk in the market and buy a piece of fish."

"It's not the same."

"What grade was your daughter in?"

"Wasn't in a grade." He turned his head until he could see Liesl. The left side of her coat and hood were covered with snow. Her eyebrows were white and her face was red from the cold. They made her eyes an even brighter blue. "We home-schooled Gretchen. She was seven."

She stared back at him and he couldn't keep his eyes on her. He turned, lowered his head against the wind, and watched his snowshoes.

They walked down the road about a half mile, then began to climb the hill. Liesl explained that in order to get up the hill they would have to zigzag, ascending very slowly. It was rough going. The woods were dense and they often had to push through branches. At times it was so steep they had to grab hold of a tree and pull themselves up to the next step. Liesl had slung her rifle over her shoulder so she could use both arms. Norman continued to lead, and occasionally he would set himself, holding a branch, then reach back and lend her a hand as she stepped up.

Once he lost his balance, and for a moment he had the gut-hollowing sensation that he was going to fall backwards and sail off the side of the hill. But he managed to fall forward awkwardly, and his arms went into the snow all the way up to his shoulders. "It's deep," he said, laughing.

Liesl had to help him to his feet. "See, you can't run away," she said. "And I wouldn't recommend trying to fly."

•

It took over an hour to reach the crest of the hill. Liesl said they should rest. She had brought some chocolate and they sat on a granite outcropping to eat. They could see down through the trees to the next smaller hill. Norman kept scanning the valley.

"Where's the road?" he asked finally. "I don't see a clearing down there."

"It's on the other side of that hill."

"You didn't mention a second hill."

"Didn't I?"

"So, it's going to be like that?" he said, nodding.

"Like what?"

"All my life it seems people tell half of what they know. I believe 'em—then suddenly they tell me there's another hill." Norman took another bite of chocolate. "What kind is this?"

"Semi-sweet. It's one of my favorite things to eat."

"We don't get this in prison."

"I used to eat a great deal, particularly in winter. Harold and I were both large people. My jaw was fractured in the accident and my mouth was wired shut for a long time. I couldn't eat solid food and I lost nearly sixty pounds. I don't eat like I used to, but in cold weather like this I love semi-sweet chocolate." She turned her head so she could see around the edge of her hood with one eye. He had the blue wool cap pulled taut over his skull so his ears were completely covered. He raised a gloved hand and tugged his cap farther down his forehead, so it came over his eyebrows. There was something about his eyes that was alert, even startled. She got out her cigarettes and after several attempts they both got one lit. "Norman, what do you mean you 'sort of' raped and beat your girlfriend?"

"I don't know what I did for certain," he said. "I was really drunk, and I'd done some stuff too, you know? No question I was whacked out. Kim and I both worked for this company that made auto parts—she worked in the office, and I was out in the warehouse driving a forklift. We got engaged, but I started to wonder, you know, if she wasn't seeing someone else. A few weeks before the wedding, I walked into her apartment and found her in bed with my brother Luke. We never got along so good. He's a couple years older and, well, we got in this shouting thing, and pushed each other around, until he left. Then I turned on her and I—I did what they say I did, I guess. I really don't remember. The rape business I don't remember at all, but I did hit her, I did shove her around, no question. She fell at some point and was knocked out, and somehow she lost sight in her right eye. The judge really went after me." He adjusted the cap around his ears. "I should have left Kim alone. If I was going to get sent away, I should have gone after my brother instead."

"Where are they now?"

"Oh, they're married and expecting their second kid."

"If you had managed to escape, I mean, to really get out of the U.P., what would you do?"

"I don't know. I didn't really have a plan. I mean, my escaping was something that I just did, right then. I'm what they call a trustee and we get to move quite freely around the prison. It's the Level Fives, the crazies, that they keep really locked up. Nobody has contact with them 'cept the guards. A bunch of us trustees were unloading supplies in the kitchen, then we were told that one of the trucks got stuck in the snow on the road out to 41, so we went outside to dig and push the thing. The snow was really coming down, and I suddenly realized I could just walk into the woods and no one would notice right off. So I did."

"You're not answering my question. Where would you go? Back down to Lansing?"

"What, get revenge? No, I'd go far away. I'd try to be someone else."

"That, Norman, is impossible to do." Liesl stood up and slung the rifle over her shoulder. "Ready? Going downhill in showshoes is tougher than climbing."

•

Norman led the way. The strain on the legs was worse and it was harder to keep balance. He often felt as though he would pitch forward and roll down the hill. He never took a step without having at least one hand on a tree trunk or branch.

They came to a trail in the snow, deep narrow tracks, frequent patches of urine, and small pellets. When they rounded a nob on the side of the hill they saw half a dozen deer standing in the snow. They were scrawny, their coats ruffled by the wind. All the deer started to move off except one, a smaller deer, which simply stood still, with its head turned toward Norman and Liesl.

She stepped past him. "Winters like this a lot of them starve. It takes a long time to do that, and they're so cold eventually they can't move. I see them around my house. They just stand there."

She walked toward the deer and stopped when she was perhaps ten yards away. The deer only watched her approach. Liesl unshouldered the rifle, took aim, and shot the deer in the chest. It fell over, blood seeping into the snow.

Norman walked up to the deer. Though its eyes were open, it was dead.

"I used to watch the weak ones die," she said, "but finally a couple of years ago I went out and shot one. Now I do it when I'm sure they're not going to make it."

"There was a photograph on the wall by your bedroom door," he said. "It's gone now." She looked at him, surprised, then curious. "It was of your husband and daughter?"

"No, it was a photograph Harold took of the Château Frontenac." Something in her eyes told him she understood. "It's a huge old hotel in Quebec City, on a cliff overlooking the St. Lawrence. We went there on our honeymoon, then we went back with Gretchen when she was five. It's odd, photographs of Harold and Gretchen aren't so bad. I have several in the bedroom. I like looking at them. I do for long periods of time. But photos of places we'd been, especially Quebec, they're much harder. Maybe it's because they were places we visited and liked, and they're still there, in the world, so to speak. Places I'll never go to again. Something like that."

"The only thing I know about Quebec is that they speak French and the Nordiques moved to Colorado and became the Avalanche."

They left the deer and continued down the hill, zigzagging slowly through the woods.

"Everything is in French," she said from above and behind him. "And the architecture is—well, I've never been to France, but it *feels* like being there. Very old buildings, many with these tall steep roofs covered with copper, which over the years has turned a bright green called verdigris."

"I've seen that," he said.

"And even if you don't speak French you quickly pick up enough to manage in shops and cafés. Some Americans complain that Quebecois pretend not to understand them. But we never encountered that. We always found them friendly. I think that when they first look at you they make a distinction—something about body language or maybe our eyes—and determine if you're American or English Canadian. If you're American and you don't walk in expecting them to speak your language, they treat you fine. And the food! All you'd do is eat, then walk, then eat, then walk some more. *Moules et frites*—mussels and French fries, that was our favorite lunch. And when you're not eating or walking you make love in a room with a view of the river—with French music on the radio."

Norman stopped and looked over his shoulder. Half of her mouth formed a smile, while the lax side hardly moved.

"Perhaps your friend Bing's wrong," she said. "Rather than thinking of tortures to forget the cold, you should think of things like good food and a long afternoon of fucking." She laughed. "Don't look so shocked, Norman, and let's get down this hill before dark."

•

They reached the bottom of the hill, crossed a narrow valley and climbed the smaller hill. It was not nearly as steep and they made good time. It was late afternoon when they descended, and below, through the trees, they could see County Road 580. They didn't talk once they saw the road, and Liesl began to worry about ending this. When Norman had first approached her outside the house, she would have shot him if he had tried anything. Now she wasn't sure she could. She wondered if he knew that.

•

As they neared the bottom of the hill, there were frequent rock ledges jutting through the snow. They were walking along the edge of one when Norman felt Liesl suddenly clutch at his arm, but she couldn't hold on, and she fell off the ledge. It was only about six feet into snow, but she lay still and looked up at him with an expression he didn't understand. He walked around the corner of the ledge, then made his way down to her. She hadn't moved. Lying in the snow, she looked like she'd been dancing, then suddenly froze in mid-step.

"It's my neck," she said. "I've had problems with it ever since the accident."

"Can you get up?"

Slowly she raised an arm toward him. "Pull."

He positioned himself over her, took her arm and helped her up out of the snow. Her body leaned against his and he held her as she breathed heavily.

"I don't know," she said, her voice shaking. "I don't think I can walk."

"It's not far to the road. I'll carry you. Let me get your shoes off."

As he crouched down, she kept both hands on his shoulders to keep herself upright. He removed his gloves and unbuckled her snowshoes—the leather straps were caked with ice, which he had to break off with his fingers. It took a long time to get her boots free of the harnesses, and his fingers were frozen. Finally, he got his gloves back on, then put his arms around the back of her legs.

"Are you sure about this?" She eased herself down as he stood up, so that she hung over his shoulder.

"I'm glad you lost those sixty pounds," he said.

"The rifle," she said. "It's way down in the snow."

"Fuck the rifle," Norman said. "Bambi'll have to starve."

He began walking. Her weight compressed the right side of his body, causing pain down through his hip and knee. It was only about fifty yards to the high snowbank on the side of the road, but he had to stop after each step and get his balance. Twice he put her down and shifted her to the opposite shoulder. When they were almost to the snowbank he lost his balance and fell forward. When he landed on top of her, she let out a cry.

"I'm sorry," he said. His face was against hers, and they both lay still, exhausted. Finally, he raised his head and looked at her. "I can't carry you any farther."

Her eyes were watery and she whispered, "Go get help." She kept one hand on his shoulder for a moment, then dropped her arm in the snow.

He couldn't get to his feet—there was nothing to push off of because his arms sank into the snow. He took off his snowshoes, crawled up the snowbank, then rolled over the other side onto the road. Standing, he could barely see the store a hundred yards to his left. There was a tractor trailer parked by the gas pumps, its taillights like beacons in the snow. He began walking, which now felt strange without the snowshoes.

•

After a while Liesl closed her eyes against the incessant snow-flakes. Cold seeped into her back and shoulders. Her arms and legs were outstretched as though she were floating on her back, and she tried to imagine a lake with the blue sky of a hot summer's afternoon above her. But it wouldn't hold, and she opened her eyes again to the snow. The cold had worked its way up into her ribcage, causing her to shiver. She closed her eyes again and saw bearded men in robes and fur hats. They spoke a foreign language and watched her with interest. She smelled grease. When the sharp thin needle stabbed into her anus, she remembered Gretchen's birth. But instead of descending, the pain ascended, moving slowly up through her bowels, her lungs, her esophagus, the back of her throat, then finally, as she opened her mouth, the warm steel slid along the end of her nose, its bloody tip stopping right before her eyes.

The You Is Understood

When one of the nuns has had enough of you for the day they send you to Sister Superior's office. Standing before her desk, your posture is a little straighter than for the other nuns, not quite at military attention, but shoulders back, chest out, hands at your sides where she can see them. Any hint of defiance will only make it worse.

Why has Sister Robert Marian sent you to the principal's office? Sister Superior asks. She often refers to herself as *the principal's office,* which makes me think that her wide oak desk, the linoleum tiles, the file cabinets, the radiator under the window behind her—all are a part of her. I also wonder what her real name is—to the students at St. Paul's, she's just Sister Superior, or as the wise guys called her, Soupy. But I assume she has a name like the other nuns, one which is both masculine and feminine. Sister Robert Marian, Sister Anne Joseph, Sister Regina Gabriel. They're French Canadian women who entered the order of the Sisters of Charity of Halifax, and for most of them it was that or stay on the farm. Now they're down here in the Boston Diocese, knocking the *Baltimore Catechism* into the heads of children named O'Fallon and Venuti. So you stand there, staring out the window behind Sister Superior (you seldom look her in the eye), admiring Monsignor Cooney's Ford parked behind the rectory, when she says, And the purpose of this visit?

The *And* is a nice touch, as though your transgression is part of the universal scheme. And on the third day of the week the Lord sent you down to Sister Superior's office to receive your just punishment. Your sins, your misery, your little life falls somewhere between eternal Darkness and Light. And the purpose of *this* visit?

Like she didn't already know. It's written all over your face. First of all, you had *not* memorized your Catechism questions (because the Bruins played in Montreal last night and you laid in bed listening to Fred Cusack's play-by-play). Then twice Sister Robert Marian warned you about snapping the elastic band against the back of Leo Mullen's neck (once during the Pledge of Allegiance, then while diagramming sentences). Finally, during morning lavatory break, Sister Robert Marian burst into the boys' (again), because Bubbles Blake squealed like a pig as he was getting pantsed. When she found Bubbles squirming on the floor, trying to get his blue corduroys up over those plump thighs, not a boy was near him. So she looked around, found me standing by one of the urinals and, because she'd had it in for me since Catechism, pulled me into the hall by the earlobe. The woman has a grip; had she not entered the order, those hands might be yanking newborn calves from their mothers' wombs.

Well? Sister Superior asks.

She pulled me out of the boys' lavatory, Sister Superior.

Why?

Brian Blake was—his pants fell down, Sister.

And you had something to do with this?

No, Sister.

At this moment I take my eyes off of Monsignor Cooney's Ford and venture a look: broad shoulders and a jaw to match, and behind the rimless glasses, hard, steady gray eyes. I stare out the window again.

Empty your pockets.

So it begins. You reach into the front pockets of your corduroys and pull out two rubber bands, a paper clip, a triangular rock that might be an arrowhead, a small black pocket knife, a button from your white shirt, a stick of Black Jack gum, and two baseball cards—Red Sox third baseman Frank Malzone and Yankees pitcher Whitey Ford, which you got in a trade for Norm Cash and Cookie Lavagetto.

With the eraser end of a yellow No. 2 lead pencil, Sister Superior sorts through these items as though she suspects they're con-taminated. She's slow, methodical, and whenever she moves her stiff white collar makes this dry sound that reminds you of snow squeaking under your boots when it's very cold out. Her No. 2 lead pencil pauses at the rock. Found while bicycling on Algonquin Hill near the Nike missile base, it could be radioac-tive. Because of the Russians we have Nike missile bases encir-cling Boston. Because of the Russians we have air raid drills. Because of the Russians Arnie Woo-Woo Ginsburg's Night Train Show on WMEX (*"Col-or Ra-di-o!"*) is frequently interrupted by The Conelrad Test. (*"This is only a test. In the case of an actual emergency, tune your dial to a Conelrad station on your radio."* The dial on my Silvertone AM has two small triangles, which indicate where the Conelrad stations are—for quick reference.) Sister Superior picks up the rock, which kind of resembles the Conelrad triangle and might be full of lethal isotopes that have a half-life of fifty thousand years, and puts it on one corner of her desk pad.

Figure it's good for two, at least.

The yellow No. 2 lead pencil then pushes aside the shirt but-ton, the baseball cards, isolating the stick of Black Jack gum.

You know there's no gum allowed in school, she says. It's bad for your teeth and it ends up on school furniture, which Mr. Gleason spends all summer removing.

Yes, Sister.

Then she takes up the pocket knife and holds it in her palm as though weighing it.

Six, easy.

You realize that knives are not allowed at St. Paul's.

Yes, Sister.

Knives are dangerous. What exactly did you plan on doing with it?

Whittle, Sister.

Whittle. Still, you know it's a suspendable offense.

No, Sister, I didn't know.

Like a magician, she makes the knife disappear into the folds of her loose black habit. I've often suspected that there are lots of secret pockets in those habits, that if you could ever actually *touch* Sister Superior's clothing you'd find all kinds of stuff she's lifted off kids: rocks, knives, slingshots, milk money, gum. I do know one thing: no one ever gets suspended from St. Paul's because disciplining pupils cannot be entrusted to their parents.

She straightens up in her chair, which creaks, then opens the drawer to her right. Slowly.

That'll be four for whatever you think you were doing in the lavatory, young man, two for the rock, and six for this exceedingly dangerous weapon.

Yes, Sister.

Twelve. The primary Catholic numbers are three, seven, ten and twelve. This time I'm getting one for each apostle.

She reaches into the drawer and pulls out a long, varnished oak paddle with a picture on one side: the picture is of a boy, bending over, his mouth open in pain; behind him stands a male teacher wearing a bowtie, who is spanking the boy's bottom with a paddle; and arcing over this tableaux in red letters: *The Board of Education.*

She nods and I remove the rest of my things from her desk and put them in my front pockets. (If I wanted I could tell her to look through Mark O'Fallon's pack of baseball cards—they'd be good for six easy.) She stands up, and without being told I turn and walk out into the hall. Opposite her door are two statues on tall pedastals, one of the Virgin Mary, the other of her Son, Jesus Christ. Between them, on the cinder block wall, is a large bronze plaque, which tells you (which *still* tells you more than forty years later) that St. Paul's Parochial School was opened in the fall of 1955 with the help of dozens of parish families. The list is alphabetical, and every name is Irish or Italian. Except mine. Ivanov. Doesn't matter that my mother is a Delany, that I have red hair and blue eyes. The name always stands out, on the plaque, on the board when one of the sisters writes it, in the air during morning roll call. At the end of mass, when the priest leads the congregation in a special prayer for peace with the Russians, I always think I'm some place I shouldn't be—like a spy. *Dear Premier*

Khrushchev, my decoded message might read, *at the end of mass they say a prayer especially for us.*

Standing before the plaque and the statues, I bend over and study the alternating flecked brown and white linoleum tiles. (Sometimes you can see faces in there—eyes, mouths, noses, which Leo Mullen says are the babies of unwed mothers tossed into the vat at the linoleum factory.) Sister Superior takes her first whack at my bottom. Twelve times, one for each apostle. Each whack is a gunshot, echoing down the hall. The multiplication table being recited in third grade hesitates, until Sister Anne Joseph resumes the chant. You know how frightening it is to be sitting in your seat, hands folded on your desk, when suddenly the whacks resound through the building. But right now I'm the one and I'd give anything to be sitting in my seat, going tight with fear. The pain radiates out from my bottom, down my legs, up into my back. My face seems to be swelling with pressure, with heat, and my eyes are filling with mist. They are *not* tears! They are *not!* It's from the leaning over, the sense that you can't get enough air into your lungs. Sister Superior has fallen into the rhythm of it now, leaning into her swing with her hips, shoulders, and upon impact a full arm extension that would make Ted Williams proud. She drives each successive whack home with slightly more vehemence, and as I silently count toward the last apostle it's clear that she's putting everything into the last few, because these are not just for my transgressions—not for pantsing Bubbles Blake (which I really didn't do, this time), or for the radioactive rock that might be an arrowhead, or even for the pocket knife—they are for all our other sins. For Mark O'Fallon's pack of baseball cards, which contains several playing cards with pictures of naked women. For the dirty word Frankie Joyce wrote in chalk on the parking lot asphalt, a simple declarative sentence that even I could diagram properly. Verb; the you is understood. For eighth grader Kevin McCarran, who paid Anna Gianella a quarter to unbutton her blouse and let him look inside. For Timmy Mullen, Leo's older brother, who paid Anna Gianella a dollar to unbutton her blouse and let him stick his hand inside. Sister Superior knows about all these sins, because Frankie was too stupid to keep the evidence—the piece of chalk—in his pocket, because Ruth Igo told about Kevin and Anna, because Maria Labadini told about Timmy and Anna after Maria had turned down Timmy's offer of fifty cents.

Then Sister Superior is through. The last apostle echoes off the cinderblock walls. After a moment I straighten up slowly. I do not turn and look at her, but I can hear her—her breathing is shallow, and there's the faintest wheeze.

Thank you, Sister.

You may return to your classroom now.

Thank you, Sister.

She goes into her office and shuts the door.

Walking is difficult. Slow. Think about the Bruins, about Teddy Green, Bronco Horvath or Leo Boivin, guys who play injured all the time. Stitches, bruises, pulled hamstrings, broken noses and fingers, charley horses. What's twelve whacks from Soupy compared to an elbow from Gordie Howe or a high stick from Rocket Richard? Think about what's inside Anna Gianella's blouse. Think about how this is only a test, about how when the Russians drop nuclear bombs on Boston, and we fire our Nike rockets at Moscow, the world will end in such red heat that we will all be reduced to radioactive cinders smaller than the fake arrowhead you found on Algonquin Hill. How that cinder will be blacker than the stick of Black Jack you were saving for recess. Think of the Virgin Mary and her Son, Jesus Christ, up on the crucifix, His head crowned with thorns, a deep wound in His side, nails driven through His hands and feet. Think in simple declarative sentences in which the you is understood. Think about something else, but keep walking, keep fighting the hot pain gripping your bottom.

You stop outside our classroom door and peer through the small window with the chicken wire in it. (Again, you wonder how they get that wire in the middle of the glass.) Everyone's standing, singing a Gregorian Chant, while Sister Robert Marian is stabbing the notes on the board with her pointer. Do you know why we have to learn this stuff? Why, when they could drop the bomb tonight? I do. We'll all turn to cinders, but when our souls go up to heaven there'll be a test. You don't pass, you don't go inside. Quote *Baltimore Catechism* questions. Diagram compound-complex sentences. Recite passages from *Evangeline.* Do your multiplication tables. Spell *fulfillment.* Which martyr showed so much courage that the Indian chief ate his heart? How did Balboa get to the Pacific? If a train leaves Boston, which is in the Eastern Time Zone, at five p.m. and travels 65 miles per hour to Chicago, which is in the Central Time Zone—questions designed to prepare you for eternal reward. If you knew what was on this test, you'd obey the sisters.

You open the door. You have to. You can't stand out there in the hall forever. Eventually somebody'll come by, probably Mr. Gleason with his pail of sawdust because another first grader threw up. You have no choice but to go into the classroom, walk carefully past Sister's desk, up your aisle over by the windows and take your place, standing beside your desk. Look at the board and join the singing of the Gregorian Chant. Sister Robert Marian's pointer makes a soft click every time she taps one of the notes on the board, which resemble hockey pucks. Listen, they weren't tears and Gregorian Chants aren't difficult; there's no harmony and hardly any melody. We drone on and on and on, until the end of the line, where we drop a half-note *down* and hold it.

Now, you turn your head and look to the right—you can get away with it because Sister's facing the board—and here we all are, our eyes angled toward you, though our heads are still straight forward and our mouths open as we sing. Our lips may form Latin syllables intended to praise the Lord, but we're really singing for you, who has suffered for all our sins. Her Son Jesus is in all of us. Yes. We honor you, we cherish you, we love you. We want to take you to our bosom and ease your pain. We have been saved. Our eyes are happy. Our smiles are joyous. Our voices rise toward heaven.

The Errand

A few weeks before he died, my father became a thief. Once I understood what he was up to, I realized that the only solution was to follow him when he left the house. It was a cold, overcast afternoon and I stood at the front door of my parents' cottage on Cape Cod, buttoning my overcoat as I watched his car pull out of the driveway. I'd give him a little time—I knew where he was headed.

"You're going out, too?" my mother asked from the kitchenette.

I didn't answer as I pulled on my hat and gloves. She knew very well what I was doing.

"You're going after him."

I opened the front door.

"Well," she said. She began almost everything she said with "well," but she could give each its own unique meaning and weight—this time it was particularly distressed; it said that we cannot avoid the inevitable. "I suppose it's not a bad idea."

If she had told me not to go, I would have closed the door and waited with her for my father to return. He had to be stopped—yet she wouldn't say exactly what she wanted me to do. It was the same way she had handled my father for over thirty years. Now that she had acknowledged my purpose, we were like conspirators, and no matter how honorable the mission, all conspiracies are shaded with guilt.

I wrapped my scarf around my neck but continued to stare through the crystaline frost patterns on the storm door. We had been having record cold weather on the Cape; it was better than 20 degrees below with the windchill factor, and even the short walk to my pickup truck required careful preparation.

When I hesitated long enough, my mother said, "Well, *go* if you're going to go." Her voice was urgent, but not unkind. I looked back at her, at how the last five years had aged her. She took her cigarettes from the pocket of my father's cardigan she'd been wearing for days. "Ben, you're only letting in the cold," she said.

I stepped outside and closed both doors behind me. The air froze my cheeks immediately and caused my lungs to ache. Above the cottage the pines swayed in the wind while my boots creaked on the packed snow. The door hinges on my truck were tight with cold and the vinyl seatcover crackled when I got in the cab. After a couple of sluggish whirs, the engine started, but I decided that tonight I would take out the battery and bring it in the house.

I drove slowly down the icy dirt road, passing summer cottages that were closed for the winter, then turned east on Route 28. There was no hurry. My father was simply going to the A & P to buy milk, bread, and ginger ale—he said that the chemotherapy treatments left a metallic taste in his mouth, so he drank ginger ale almost constantly. I was following him because of the cashews and instant coffee. While he was napping that afternoon, my mother had shown me the jars of Maxim and Planter's hidden behind the cereal boxes on the top shelf of the kitchen cabinets. "He's got more out in the shed," she said. She appeared alarmed, something I'd thought no longer possible. For over five years the doctors had been preparing us, telling us what we could expect—but *this* no one could anticipate. She whispered, "When I found a can in the glove compartment yesterday, I said to him, 'Why are you buying all this stuff? There's enough here to last years.' And he said, 'I didn't buy 'em, I clipped 'em.'"

And I smiled as I said, "Well, you know he's an honest man."

It was perhaps a quarter of a mile to the A & P, and I kept the truck in third gear. Both sides of the road were bordered by snowbanks. There was no one outside, not even at the gas station. Nothing moved except the street signs that fluttered in the wind. I turned on the radio, loud: at the cottage there was so much whispering and silence while my father slept that such trips from the house were also an excuse to do *something,* even if it was to just make noise. Anything to escape the sense of confinement. Before I left the house I always put a bottle of beer in each of my coat pockets. I dug one out now, unscrewed the cap, and tossed it on the floor.

At the A & P, I turned into the parking lot, where about a dozen cars were clustered near the front door. Hitting the brakes, I sent the truck into a slow skid on the packed snow. There were only two green cars, neither one the sun-faded green of my father's Dodge. I swore out loud, then turned the truck around and got back on the road.

My mother feared for the children and old people. Her logic was always so seamless, even now when it projected into the future. After she had shown me the coffee and cashews in the kitchen cabinets, she said, "With the sidewalks buried beneath snow, people have to walk in the street. And his eyesight's so bad now. How many times has he knocked over a glass of ginger ale since you've been down here?"

My father had been a salesman all his adult life and he loved to be out on the road. You couldn't mention a town in the six New England states that he didn't know; the road was where he had earned his keep for over thirty years. Now I was supposed to take that away from him. "Mom, you know what driving means to him. How do you tell him he can't drive any more? He goes down to the store and comes right back. It isn't two minutes each way, and he doesn't do better than twenty miles an hour."

My mother's eyes were moist and weary; they'd been that way for days. "But sometimes he takes so long," she said. "If he ran over someone—then where will I be? A widow with a lawsuit."

The road was covered with packed snow and ice. Even as I entered downtown Chatham there were few cars out, and no one was walking. Many of the stores had closed for the season, their owners spending six months operating another shop or restaurant in Florida. In their imagined retirement my parents had hoped to go south for the winter, like many New Englanders.

Instead, my father had been fighting lymphoma since he was fifty-five, and they now lived year-round in a small summer cottage with central heating that was inadequate during the winter. I finished my beer, wondering if rather than following my father I was chasing him. There is an essential difference. The village stores and street lamps were strung with Christmas lights, but the shoveled sidewalks were not crowded—people shopped at the malls in Hyannis and Orleans now. Only the Ben Franklin Five-and-Ten showed any real activity behind its bright window displays. I turned down the lane and entered the parking lot behind the store. My father's car wasn't there. At the far end of the lot a backhoe was loading snow into a dump truck.

As I circled back to the lane, I suddenly felt warm, not only because heat had finally filled the cab but because a real fear had struck me: if my father had gone Christmas shopping at one of the malls, I would never catch up with him. At the top of the lane I didn't come to a complete stop because of the ice—the grade was steep and my truck might slide backwards. Turning right, I heard a horn to my left and watched a car glide to a halt just a couple of feet from my door. I waved to the driver, a woman wearing white earmuffs, and mouthed "Sorry."

My father's car was not parked anywhere along the main street in the village. I considered going into the Mayflower Shop to look at magazines, or stopping at The Squire for a drink. Either would have helped me avoid what I ought to do: turn around and go home. Return to the cottage and tell my mother I'd lost my father, then sit with her while we waited. But there were so many real worries, I couldn't suffer the imagined ones with her. We had sat together in hospital waiting rooms and doctors' offices so often, that to return empty-handed and have to sit through her imagined worries about car accidents, stricken pedestrians, and lingering lawsuits was unthinkable.

Taking the beer from my other coat pocket, I drove out toward the lighthouse. This was the oldest part of town and the houses, many of them saltboxes with shingles weathered to a luminescent silver, seemed at once bleak yet proud. In spring the drive-

ways of crushed shells were bordered by an abundance of wild
roses. The road along the bay began to rise gently as it curved
toward the lighthouse. Gusts of wind coming off the ocean pushed
the truck toward the snowbank—it felt like steering against a
strong centrifugal force.

At the lighthouse the road leveled off and fanned out to the
left, broadening into the parking lot at the edge of the bluff. I
began to turn into the lot, then suddenly jerked the truck back so
quickly the rear tires slid momentarily, and I continued past the
lighthouse. My father was sitting in his car, parked by the stairs
that led down to the beach. I kept driving and took the first road
after the lighthouse, just to get out of sight; then I turned around
and drove slowly back toward the parking lot. Fearing my approach might even be heard, I shut off the radio. I stopped next
to a row of evergreen bushes, put the truck in neutral, and pulled
up the handbrake.

The bay was choppy and the wind brought the constant roar of
the surf in from North Beach. I conserved my beer as I watched
the back of my father's head. He had started to go bald by his
early twenties, and despite his wool hat the particular roundness
of his skull was unmistakable. I could look at the silhouette of a
dozen bald men and pick out my father immediately. He was
one of those men who looked like they should be bald. Five years
earlier, during the first round of chemotherapy, he had begun to
lose the little hair that remained on the sides and back of his
head, and each night he would lay his shirt or sweater out on the
bed and with a clothes brush remove the loose hair that clung to
the fabric. That we understood, for he had always been meticu-
lous—as are most men who have served in the military. But then
he went out and bought a toupee, an awful blue-gray thing with
a wedge-like part on one side. He wore it only once, at Thanks-
giving; though my mother, brothers and sister all claimed to like
it, he must have seen otherwise. For days the wig sat on top of
the lampshade on his nightstand, like some animal pelt; then it
simply disappeared. I suspect that he thought the toupee might
keep his hair from falling on his shirts, and never once consid-

ered how ridiculous it would look on his head.

As the winter light faded my father's car started to turn gray. The lighthouse beacon came on, a double strobe running along North Beach in the dusk. I rejected the notion of leaving my truck, crossing the windswept lot and joining him. I was certain it would cause embarrassment for both of us. We would feel exposed and vulnerable. Why are you here? Why are *you* here? It was one thing to spy; another to intrude. Yet some of our best talks had taken place in cars. It seemed we were always driving to or from a hockey rink, my goalie equipment smelling of sweat and leather in the heat of the car. In those days my father wore felt fedoras and smoked Chesterfields in a cigarette holder—I have never been able to look at a photograph of FDR without seeing my father. We talked about hockey or the boys on my team or something that had happened at school. We talked about me.

Except once, and I've always wondered if he planned it, or if it was something that he just felt like telling me at that time. Whichever, it seemed appropriate. It was the night I took my driver's test, which I had passed easily, and my father let me drive home from the registry. He told me about his older brother Ben. He said that I always reminded him of Ben: he'd been athletic, something of a prankster, and never interested in school. He and my father grew up in Brooklyn until the Crash of '29 wiped out their father's trucking business. Their mother took them back to her family's home in the Mohawk Valley in Upstate New York, believing it would be easier to raise them in the country, while their father continued to look for work in the city. My father said that in their teens he and his brother would take any job, and there were times when they had raided a garden or chicken coop. Neither graduated from high school; Ben got married the year he would have been a senior, and my father was expelled for what he called "a little scrape." They were both musicians: Ben played the piano and my father tenor saxophone, and in the years prior to the war they played in jazz bands in clubs from Albany to Syracuse. My father said that Ben might have made it as a professional; he was that good. When the Japanese attacked Pearl Harbor, they both enlisted, and they didn't see each other until the war was over five years later. Amid the first days of celebration upon their return home, it was clear that Ben was not the same—he'd been in some very bad fighting in the South Pacific. He didn't get along with his wife, which was nothing new, but he was sullen in a way my father had never seen before. Sitting in the passenger seat while I drove home from the registry, my father said quietly, "So he got drunk and took an overdose of sleeping pills. Then he went out and ran his car into a tree. He lost it, that's all." Getting my driver's license was a step toward independence, which I desperately wanted, and my father rewarded me with a story about my uncle's suicide drive.

A seagull landed on the hood of my truck and I held perfectly still, the beer bottle tucked between my thighs. The gull looked around, its head stopping intermittently, as if photographing each direction. Its indifferent eye resembled a smooth black button; the gray wings and white breast mimicked the overcast sky. A gust of wind shook the truck and the gull rose into the air, beat across the parking lot, soared above the bluff, then dove in an arc toward the bay. After a moment my father backed his car up and pulled out into the road. I let out the handbrake and put the truck in gear.

I gave him about a hundred yards as we wound down toward the village. The street lights were on now and it was almost dark. A truck passed me going the other way, and the driver, a hefty, bearded man, raised his hand from the steering wheel and spread his fingers in greeting. Though I didn't recognize him, I returned the gesture; it was a custom we had up in Newburyport, where I lived—guys in trucks in small towns naturally assume some kind of affinity. But as I waved back I imagined a darkening coastal town full of young men in trucks shadowing their fathers.

Almost as if he knew he was being observed, my father drove slowly back through the village and toward the A & P. When he entered the market parking lot, I pulled over in front of the post office. I waited in the truck and turned on the radio again; the news said there would be no break in the cold front and there was a severe fuel shortage on Cape Cod. As a result, municipal buildings were being closed, and the Red Cross was asking for contributions of coats, blankets and food, to be stored in churches and schools on the Cape. In Boston, the governor had announced that an emergency shipment of heating oil was heading north, and the tanker, which was presently off the Carolinas, should arrive within days. There was something quaint and ironic about all this—Cape Cod, Nantucket and Martha's Vineyard awaiting a lone ship plying the sea lanes with a cargo of twentieth century whale oil.

My father emerged from an aisle carrying bread and a half-gallon of milk against his chest. He had the look of a man who was doing his part. His face wasn't grim so much as determined. I couldn't tell whether he was concealing anything beneath his bulky coat, but suddenly I hoped he was: like an animal, he was laying in provisions, not for the winter, but for after he was gone. His logic was twisted—there certainly was no need for more instant coffee and cashews, and he could afford to pay for them—but the instinct was right.

There was a problem at the check-out counter. The teenaged boy behind the register leaned away from my father as he began gesturing with his arms. The boy must have said something about shoplifting. I got out of the truck and hurried across the parking lot toward the store. The wind coming around the corner of the building seemed to prolong my walk, my body bent forward and my chin tucked into my scarf. I would simply pay for anything my father had stolen and offer no excuses. If the boy tried to make an issue of it, if he called for the store manager, I would take my father by the arm and walk him out the door. Nobody was going to chase us out into this cold. When I entered the store, pennants strung between the ceiling lights fluttered madly in the wind.

My father turned around and looked up—he was angry and he didn't appear surprised to see me. "They're out of Canada Dry!" he said, trying to raise his hoarse voice. His teeth were chipped and gray, and the blood blister under his lower lip bobbed up and down as he spoke.

"Deliveries are slow because of the weather," the boy said apologetically. "I suggested another brand."

"I don't *want* another brand!"

"What was wrong with that White Rock I bought the other day?" I asked. My father just stared at me. "Got it on sale," I added.

"My whole life I've been looking for bargains," he said, "and now I'm through with 'em. That White Rock stuff, I poured it down the kitchen sink. Both quarts. Didn't taste right."

I looked at the boy, who shrugged his shoulders. "Has he paid you for everything?"

The boy nodded, then quickly put the milk and bread in a paper bag.

"What are you doing here?" My father asked, picking up the bag.

"Mom needed bay leaves for her spaghetti sauce."

"Bullshit." My father started for the door. He walked quickly; he wasn't waiting for me. I was part of the conspiracy, along with my mother, the young sales clerk and, most likely, the doctors in Boston. When I caught up, he said, "You've been following me."

"Mom's been worried. You've been gone a long time."

He stopped at the door and looked at me. Under the bright lights his skin was yellow, and his eyes were the dull white of a hard-boiled egg. "When I left the lighthouse I saw you in my mirror. How long were you there?"

"Most of the time. You lost me at first."

"And you thought to look at the lighthouse?"

"Well, yeah, I did. I'm glad you go out there."

"I'm going to be cremated and buried out there." My father leaned his shoulder against the door. "I'm going to leave this weather far behind, *way* behind. Trust me."

As he pushed the door open against the wind, something fell out from under his overcoat. We both stared down at the jar of cashews, lying in the slush. Suddenly I felt very warm—we were going to get caught. I didn't dare look back into the store for fear that the manager would be bearing down on us. I kicked the jar out of the doorway, and it rattled across the ice and concrete until it landed in a dingy snowbank. Taking my father's arm, we moved quickly out into the wind, across the parking lot.

"Is that it?" I asked. "You got any more under there?"

My father shook his head.

We were going to get away with it and I was suddenly elated. I think he was, too.

"Listen to me," I said.

"What?" He knew what was coming—I was sure of it.

"You can't drive any more."

He turned his head away. "Your mother put you up to this."

"Not really."

"Well, I don't like it."

"Any place you want to go, I'll drive you."

"Any place?"

"Any place."

He looked at me then. "Well, I'm not sorry."

"I know."

The wind was at our backs, and when a gust came up we were almost running. When we reached his car I held the door open for him. The wind was really up.

"Okay?" I had to shout.

"Okay!"

I jogged to my truck parked by the post office, expecting him to head home without me, but when I got in behind the wheel I saw that his car was waiting by the exit. I started my engine, turned on the lights, and he led me home through the dark.

Disciple Pigeons

Marsha could barely squeeze into her phone booth. It was the stupid door's fault, folding in the middle like that. As she struggled to get change from her bluejeans she considered moving again. Maybe someplace up in Balboa Park that would provide room for her newspapers and LeBag. But at night the cops patrolled the park for winos and sex offenders. Maybe down by the Santa Fe Depot, near the harbor. Anything would be better than living in this phone booth on A Street. She put one foot up on her stack of newspapers and dropped coins into the payphone.

Each operator seemed more distant, the third one clearly Italian. "I want the Vatican," Marsha said loudly.

There was no response, only static. Last week when she had called, the connection was so bad the operator couldn't even hear her—and after Marsha had hung up it took three more calls to get her money back, going right up to an assistant manager named Mrs. Balfour.

"The Vatican?" the operator asked, sounding as if she were under water. "Which office?"

Marsha looked down A Street toward the wedge of water and sky between tall buildings. The bow of a destroyer slid out of the glass wall on the left, and a jet plane spread a trail of dark smog as it rose above the harbor, taking today's divorcees to Reno. It was almost 7 a.m. here in San Diego, but she wasn't sure what time it was in Rome. "The Papal Office," she said.

The static changed; it became louder, more distinct, and Marsha imagined one of those quick scenes from an old movie where we were always fighting the Nazis and the telephone operator, in curls and padded shoulders, plugged the phone jack into the socket after saying, "I'll connect you." The destroyer, its stern now in view and fanning out a pearly wake, was going out on maneuvers against the communists.

"Hello," a man said. "Father Bardino speaking." Last week her call had been answered by a priest who sounded older and French. Had the older one warned Father Bardino about her?

"Father, I wish to leave a message."

"Yes?" He seemed confused. Innocent. Why wasn't he in Africa or India doing good works? "What is it?"

She wouldn't make the same mistake this week. No one, even a bishop or a cardinal, simply calls and gets the pope on the line. You have to schedule an appointment.

"I wish for the Holy Father to return my call, at his convenience, of course." Slow down. "It. Is. Very. Important."

"The Holy Father?"

"Yes, the Pope."

Father Bardino paused and there was a muffled sound. He was probably holding the receiver against his young chest and telling the older priest from France, "It's her again."

The priest cleared his throat. "Please, who's calling?"

"This is Sister Marsha, calling from San Diego, California, United States. Of America. If He would just call me at—" she read the number on the payphone—"I will give Him the message."

"Sister, what order are you in?"

"Please, He must return my call."

"You must realize—"

"Tell Him I'll be waiting." She hung up, took her portable radio out of her LeBag and walked quickly away from her phone booth before the operator could call asking for more change to be deposited.

•

Sitting in Balboa Park she listened to Ted on the radio. She fed the last of her popcorn to the pigeons around her sneakers. A kernel had embedded itself behind a molar and she dug at it with her tongue. One pigeon, with a neck that glistened purple and blue like an oil slick, ate the last of the popcorn and followed the others across the grass to a Mexican woman who was breaking up a loaf of whole wheat bread. Marsha's mouth secreted painfully, but at last the kernel worked loose, leaving a raw spot in her gum that tasted of sweet, salty blood. The radio program was called The Word. "I do love you, Ted," she whispered.

Ted took another caller, a woman named Regina from Escondido. Her six-year-old son had been digging a hole in the backyard when he was attacked by a swarm of yellow jackets. His body was covered with bee stings; they had gotten up under his Chargers T-shirt, and even his eyelids were swollen shut.

"And what did you do, Dear?" Ted asked.

Watching the whole wheat arc from the Mexican woman's hand to the oil slick pigeon's beak, Marsha was suddenly jealous. Ted had called her Dear over the radio, too.

"Well," Regina explained, sounding Panhandle or West Texas, "I'm alone, Ted, being three years divorced and never having taken anything more than food stamps either, and my boyfriend Bobby—he's a fireman—was on duty, so I didn't know what to do but to take my little boy in my arms, fall down on my knees and pray to the Lord."

Slut, Marsha thought as she watched the Mexican woman brush her hands off, creating a dervish among her disciple pigeons. Marsha's children, Ricardo and Inez, lived in Nevada with her mother, safe from any swarming bees.

"God bless you, child," Ted whispered. "And the boy's pain?"

Marsha turned off the radio. "Of course it's gone, completely."

The Mexican woman looked at her, then down at her empty, whole wheat hands and said, *"Si."*

•

Marsha waited outside her phone booth, shielding her eyes from the sun. The glare off the smooth harbor between the buildings had turned from white to gold. In minutes the sun would set behind Point Loma, turning the water pink and the sky orange, then just before darkness, purple.

Papal purple.

Ted was late.

He didn't show last week either, though he had promised. This time, when she had called The Word after Regina and all those busy signals because the operators wouldn't put the right jack in the proper socket, Ted said he remembered her, though she knew he didn't.

Though he said, "How are you, Dear?"

"My children live in Nevada with my mother," Marsha said, hearing her voice on her radio, "because of my ex-husband Ricardo, the things he forced me to do."

"God be with you, Dear," Ted said quickly, and a commercial came on the radio, claiming that soup was good food.

"It's you again," Ted said into her phone.

Marsha turned off her radio. "Yes, Dear. My love for you is real, and the things I did for Ricardo I want to do for you, though now they would be acts of love."

•

The western sky over Point Loma was purple. The man walked up A Street, looking as though he were lost.

Marsha stepped out of her phone booth. "Hello Ted."

He stared at her Padres T-shirt.

"Hungry?"

"Whatever you want," she said.

He turned and hailed a Yellow Cab.

•

It was her third paper plate of the free hors d'oeuvres. The bar in the Gaslamp Quarter had a white tile floor and a large stained glass dome in the ceiling. Outside, there was a doorman dressed as a bobby, and across the street sailors leaned against the front windows of a card room. Two black women in leather skirts worked the corner. Marsha finished the breaded chicken wing, licked her fingers and picked up a piece of cauliflower. "It was a matter of citizenship," she said, "not marriage."

Ted's worried eyes checked the patrons down the bar. He had a habit of brushing the corduroy on his coat sleeve the wrong way.

"You're recognized frequently," she said. "It must be haunting."

A white Shore Patrol van passed by slowly.

Ted sipped his beer. "It's not a problem on radio. Only if you're on TV."

"I remember when you did the weather on KBDK."

"Really? That was a while ago."

"Yes, I remember that Christmas story they all did on you."

"You do?"

"You were at some mall making a public appearance and you took a swing at Santa Claus."

"I dried out after that," he said. "You're from San Diego?"

"I've always lived here, except for the six months in Mexico City," she said, running a piece of broccoli through the onion dip. "You were thinner then. We have that in common."

He glanced down at her Padres. "I wouldn't call you fat."

She leaned closer and whispered, "Have you ever noticed how if you close your eyes cauliflower and broccoli both taste exactly the same?"

•

The hotel room was small. Marsha could sit on the edge of the bed and lean out the open window.

"Jesus, put something on," Ted said. "You want the police up here?"

She tickled the sole of his foot until he pulled it away. "You have such a calm voice on the radio." She smiled at him.

"Motels are safer." He laid back and stared at the ceiling. "They're cleaner, more anonymous."

"I thought it wasn't a problem on the radio."

"People die in hotels like this."

"People die everywhere."

"All right," he said. "But they get killed down here."

Marsha began emptying her LeBag on the bed.

Ted sat up and watched. "You looking for something in particular?" He sorted through the pile: a shoehorn, a notebook, pliers, an aluminum pot, a bottle of detergent, one mitten, a ball of twine.

She found the can of cream of celery soup. "I need my opener."

"What, do you live out of this bag?"

"I have a place on A Street." She found the opener and picked up the aluminum pot. "Don't worry, I don't have a gun in here."

She went to the sink and turned on the hot water, then opened the can and mixed the soup and water in the aluminum pot. "See my spoon anywhere on the bed, Dear?"

Looking up she saw Ted pulling on his boxers.

"I'm late," he said.

"But aren't you hungry?"

"No thanks. Had a big lunch."

"Your show isn't until morning. We can do anything you want. Anything, Ted. With you they're acts of love."

"I really can't stay."

She stared at his appendix scar.

"I'm expecting a phone call," he said.

"We all are. I should hear from the Pope today."

"Well," he said, leaning over to gather up his slacks, "give Him my best."

"You don't mean that."

"I do."

"It's Regina, isn't it."

"Who?"

"Your phone call. That slut, with her boyfriend on duty at the fire station."

Ted had one leg in his pants, the other raised like a flamingo. "Listen, Honey, I'm not even Catholic."

"Don't call me 'Honey.'"

The cream of celery soup arced across the room and splattered on his chest. Ted screamed and Marsha rushed to him, fell to her knees and licked the hot liquid from his appendix scar.

•

Though her eyelids were swollen, she could feel the morning sunlight. The bedsheet under her hand and cheek was stiff, and when she got her eyes open she could see that it was dried blood.

Everything hurt.

Beyond the articles from her LeBag, she saw them; bills, one-hundred dollar bills; two, no three of them.

There was a knock on the door. She sat up quickly, gasping as she saw her face in the mirror above the sink.

"Eleven o'clock," a woman said. "Es checkout time."

•

Soup

Bread

Bird seed

She looked up from her list at an old black man with the trombone case. He wore a tuxedo and a white ruffled shirt with pearl buttons that matched his teeth.

"Hey, Darlin'?"

She looked down and wrote on her list.

Peanutbutter

Tampons

Tunafish

"Yo' eyes, what ha'm?" His trombone case was patched with gray duct tape.

"Bee sting," she said through sore lips. "I'm allergic."

"Sheet."

People were still streaming across the park toward the rally at Sixth and Laurel. The candidate's PA-voice echoed off the buildings.

"You play in that jazz band?" she asked.

"That's right."

"Who's speaking now, the president?"

"Naw. Jus' some local dude," he said. "I don't follow politics."

"Me neither," Marsha said, getting up slowly. "I'm a religious person myself."

"I could see that." He picked up her LeBag and handed it to her.

"I'm Sister Marsha."

"Uh-huh. Lionel. Pleased to make your acquaintance, Sister."

"You headed downtown?"

"Uh-huh."

"Come on, Lionel," she said, taking a hundred dollar bill from her bluejeans. "God has been good to me. I'll buy you a bus ride."

•

"You live here or some'm?"' Lionel asked, looking at the stack of newspapers in the phone booth on A Street.

"I'm a native San Diegan," Marsha said, "not one of these germy people come from the north every winter."

He looked down A Street toward the harbor and squinted. "Say all I got to do is call the man? And jus' read this message?" The notebook page rattled against his leg. The satin stripe running down his trousers puckered where the thread was missing.

Marsha nodded as she dialed again. The phone rang once, then she heard Ted's voice, through the receiver as well as on her portable radio. She slid out of the booth so Lionel could get in. He tried to close the door, but she stopped it with her foot.

"Hello," Ted said, "You're on the air."

Lionel cleared his throat. "Ted," he said, holding the notebook page up. "'Soup, bread, bird seed—'"

"Sir?" Ted asked.

Lionel looked farther down the notebook page. "I mean, uh, 'Marsha is dying and if you want to save her life you must get the Pope to call the following number at seven p. m. today.'" He read the phone booth number.

Ted sort of laughed.

Lionel glanced at Marsha as she waved quick circles in the air with her hand. Staring at the notebook page again, he continued, "'Otherwise, you will read your obituary in the newspaper.'" He recited the telephone number again, then hung up carefully.

"Hello there," Ted said over the radio. *"Sir?"*

"Right," Lionel said to Marsha. "Allergies."

•

From the tenth deck of the Community Concourse Garage Marsha could see the entire harbor. Planes drifted in low over Balboa Park and landed at the airport; a destroyer passed under the Coronado Bridge, headed for the 32nd Street Naval Station. When the western sky was in its final stage of orange, the first lights came on along Point Loma.

She took the elevator down to ground level and walked slowly up to A Street, changing her heavy LeBag from arm to arm. The problem was where to store the five pounds of bird seed; it had to be some place where no one would look and the birds couldn't get at it. *There was no place on this earth like that.* Thank God she had buried the peanut butter and tuna fish under a eucalyptus tree in Balboa Park or she'd never make it to her phone booth on time.

•

The phone rang exactly at seven p. m.

"Hello?"

"Sister Marsha?"

"Yes."

"This is the Pope."

Marsha looked down A Street at the dark harbor, its reflected city lights. "Really, Ted. Your accent's not bad, but the Pope's not Italian."

After a moment, Ted said in his own voice, "I've called to save your soul, Sister Marsha."

"And your reputation."

"Amen." Ted took a long, deep breath, like he often did on his radio program. It always preceded those moments when he was about to speak The Word. "What is it you want, Dear?" he whispered. "I'll give you anything. They are all acts of love."

Night Train To Chicago

As the train pulled out of the East Lansing station, I noticed that my hands were shaking again. I glanced at my reflection in the window, where snow blew so hard against the dark glass that it might have been sand. Only my forehead, cheekbones and nose really caught the light, and my hair appeared to be the color of pencil lead. I might have been looking at a grainy black and white photograph, a composite of shadows. It was the kind of man's face that people would find difficult to describe. No scars. No prominent features. If I were missing or perhaps a suspect in a crime, witnesses would have a hard time recalling any distinguishing characteristics.

"I prefer trains," an old woman seated behind me said. There was something labored in her speech, and I suspected that she wore dentures. Or possibly she was drunk. "Haven't taken a plane since I was on one that nearly crashed."

I glanced over my shoulder. She was in her seventies and she was looking toward the window, talking to herself. Brown over-coat, plaid scarf, and a yellow wool hat pulled tightly down on her skull.

"Have you ever been frightened," she asked without looking from the window, "while at the same time you were marveling at something beautiful?" I faced toward the front of the passenger car. "On our honeymoon," she continued, "my husband Joseph and I went to Niagara Falls. We took this boat, *Maid of the Mist,* right up to the bottom of the falls." I was tempted to turn around again and tell her I'd taken the same tour. "We put on these rain slickers with hoods. That's what makes it special, I think. Every-body crammed on the deck in these yellow slickers while the boat steams toward the falls. Like we were headed straight for disaster! But people were laughing, yelling. Children screaming. Then the boat was *right* next to the falls! We were getting drenched, and the water—it was an absolute *roar!*—tons of water, falling constantly. Then Joseph shouts in my ear, '*Look at that rainbow!*' It was there above us, and I was never so frightened, staring up at that beautiful rainbow."

I stood up, nearly losing my balance against the sway of the train, and started up the aisle. My legs were shaky, and I had to take hold of the backs of seats and pull myself forward. It had begun as a slight tremor, like a faint hum, that seemed to run through my entire body; then, several weeks ago, I had paused during a meeting at work and looked at my hand. I made a fist several times just to prove that I had some control over my fingers. The meeting was ending and the others were getting up from the table. Only Carolyn Ducette seemed to notice what I was doing. It had been a particularly long and contentious meeting, and her cheeks were flushed as a result of an argument we'd had over next year's budget. I never liked arguing with her about policy, but this session had been particularly difficult since we had recently stopped seeing each other.

When I reached the concession stand there wasn't anything to hold on to and the train was going around a bend, so I had to lean to my left. Then the car righted itself and I took a step forward to avoid stumbling. Someone fell against my back, and for a moment an arm came around my waist, and a hand took hold of my wrist. Looking down, I saw the hand retreat quickly. A woman's hand, slender fingers and nails with clear polish.

"Sorry," she whispered and I turned around. She was in her late thirties, wearing an olive-green beret and a black turtleneck sweater. Taking hold of the bottom of my overcoat, she began patting the wool with a paper napkin. "That last jolt—I'm afraid I spilled my coffee on you."

"Don't worry about it."

She continued to daub the fabric with the napkin, which had turned brown and soggy. "Here," she said taking hold of my sleeve and leading me down the aisle, "my seat's right here and I have some bottled water—"

She sat down and didn't let go of my sleeve until I sat beside her. Rummaging through a backpack on the floor, she found a blue plastic bottle of water and a handkerchief. After soaking the handkerchief, she went to work and there was something intimate about the way she handled the bottom of my coat. Her fingers pulled and stretched the fabric, careful to get all of the coffee stain. I saw in her open backpack a copy of Joan Didion's *Slouching Towards Bethlehem.*

"You're a grad student?" I asked.

"Was a grad student." For the first time she raised her head and stared at me. Her brown eyes were large and she seemed worried. "A year ago I realized that what the world *doesn't* need is one more doctoral candidate in English. Of course, that's the easy part—it's figuring out what the world *does* need that's hard." She put the handkerchief away, then turned and glanced toward the back of the train. I liked her shoulders and the way the heavy turtleneck sweater encircled her throat. Turning, she slid down in her seat and whispered, *"God,* I knew it."

"Knew what?"

"Paul's on the train."

I looked toward the back of the train. Many of the passengers appeared to be students, most of them in their twenties. There was one man with a graying beard and his collar turned up, who stared straight forward, as though in a trance. "In the peacoat?" I asked, turning around again.

"Follows me everywhere."

"Even to Chicago?"

"That's why I'm going," she said, neatly folding up her damp handkerchief. "In Chicago I thought I'd be able to look around and *not* see him there for once."

"What is he, an old boyfriend? Husband? Stalker?"

"You got it, all in one shot." She smiled at me, revealing one slightly crooked front tooth. "You must have an advanced degree. Several even, to figure that out. Paul has all his degrees. He figures it all out. It can drive you crazy. He's the last Ph.D. that the world will *ever* need. You have a Ph.D.?"

"No."

"Good. People with doctorates are different from you and me."

"The husband part," I said. "He's a husband, but not your husband."

She leaned back to get a better look at me. "Boy, you're *good.*" She took a sip of water from the blue bottle, which she then put in her backpack.

"Is he dangerous?"

"At the moment?" She straightened up, drawing a strand of blond hair off her mouth. "Hard to say." Then she smiled again, though there was no joy in her eyes. "You'd have to define dangerous."

It seemed like a challenge, possibly even a dare. "That which you don't know," I said.

"Okay. As definitions go, okay. Why are you going to Chicago?"

"I don't know," I said. "I really don't."

"That's not only dangerous, it's mysterious," she said. "You're not meeting anyone? No planned assignation?"

"I have no plans at all. Really."

"You're just *going,*" she said reverentially.

"It feels pretty desperate, actually," I said.

"I suppose it depends on whether you're running toward something or running away. In my case I'm doing both, I think."

"Perhaps I'm doing neither."

"*That's* desperate."

"Maybe," I said. "You spilled your coffee. Would you like another?" She stared at me as though I had asked her the most personal question imaginable. I didn't know what that question would be, but I wished I did. I realized that I hadn't been shaking since I'd sat down with her. "I could go for some," I said. "How do you want yours?"

"Black."

As I stood in the aisle, I glanced toward the back of the train car. Paul still appeared to be in a trance. I went forward to the concession stand. There were no other customers now and I asked the young black man for two coffees. It occurred to me that this woman in the beret might have spilled her first coffee on me intentionally, just to get me to sit with her, as protection from this man in the back of the car. I wondered if I was allowing myself to be drawn into the middle of something I didn't fully understand. She had a way of establishing need and trust and familiarity immediately, and no doubt men often wanted to make themselves useful to her.

I paid for the two coffees, picked up the styrofoam cups and turned around—Paul was standing right behind me. He had the kind of dead-on stare that some boys develop early in life. No one ever challenges them; only fools pick fights with them outside of school.

"Excuse me," I said, stepping to Paul's right. Then I stopped, looking down the aisle: the young woman was gone—only her coat lay open in her seat.

"You know she's crazy," Paul said. The man had gray eyes. They seemed now to be trying to reach me, which made them difficult to look away from—there was a desperation, a weariness, even a fear in them that seemed genuine. He leaned closer, and before he spoke I could smell hot chocolate in his beard. "She does this more and more frequently, running off to Chicago," he said, barely a whisper above the clatter of the train. "I don't know what to do anymore."

"I'm sorry?" Paul was wearing a gold stud in his right earlobe and I forced myself to look at it. But it didn't work, and I had to come back to the eyes.

"Listen," he said, "it's just too late." Then he turned and walked toward the front of the passenger car and entered one of the lavatories.

•

Lately the arguments at work had become more frequent and,

at times, more personal. Before Carolyn and I agreed to stop seeing each other, we had begun to bring the arguments away from work with us. So they were continued in restaurants, in line at the movies, at dinner parties. When we started to argue about work in bed I think we both knew it was over. She often reminded me that we were bureaucrats—state government bureaucrats—and that our first loyalty should be to the public, that the decisions we made regarding policy really affected people. I maintained that I understood that, and, in fact, suggested that many of my decisions were based on that realization—including those decisions which, on the face of it, appeared to have a detrimental effect on people. Men, women and children, she said. Citizens, I said, people who pay taxes and expect their money to be spent responsibly, people who understand that hard decisions made now might help avoid difficulties in the future.

The heat from the coffee was coming through the styrofoam and I placed the cup on the counter. The young black man was reading a magazine and he didn't look up.

"I was wondering," I said, and waited till the young man raised his eyes. His hair was close cropped and there was a faint diagonal part that ran in from the right temple. "The woman in the beret, sitting right back there—have you seen where she's gone?"

The young man nodded his head toward the front of the car, then continued with his magazine.

I left the coffee on the counter and made my way up to the lavatories. Paul had gone into the one on the right. The one on the left was also occupied, but turning so my back was to the concession stand, I said quietly through the door, "You all right?"

After a moment the latch was thrown and the door opened. She stared out at me and there was something different about her face—she'd either been crying, or she'd washed it. Her skin, which had been very pale, was now flushed, and her eyes were moist. She reached out, took hold of my coat collar and pulled me into the lavatory. When the door was closed behind me, she was pressed up against me, so close I could smell shampoo in her hair.

"Listen," I said. She raised her face to me. We were close enough to kiss. "I spoke with Paul."

"You did?"

"Well, he spoke to me at the concession stand and—"

Suddenly, the train began to slow down. My haunches were thrust against the sink, and she fell hard into me. The train continued to slow and her face was pressed into my neck. There was the screech of metal just before the car stopped. Then the lights flickered and went out. It was pitch black in the lavatory.

She lifted her head off my neck. It was like when she'd cleaned the coffee stain—everything about her was familiar. Here in the dark she leaned against me like a lover. "Are you all right?" she whispered.

"I'm warm," I said.

Her arms came up and she helped me work my coat off my shoulders. The lavatory was so small that the coat simply laid behind me, against the wall. "That better?" She kept her arms on my shoulders.

"Yes," I said. "Thanks."

•

"Ladies and gentlemen," a voice said loudly from the front of the car. "We're sorry for the delay, but we're having mechanical problems due to the blizzard. We'll get underway as soon as possible."

"They could at least turn on the lights," she whispered. "Must be electrical problems." Then she pressed closer and her warm, damp cheek rested against my neck. "Then again," she said, her voice husky and playful, "maybe we're better off?"

"Would you rather return to your seat?" I asked.

"Where's Paul?"

"He went into the other lavatory."

"I don't dare go out there in the dark."

She was holding me tightly now. My hands had been gripping

the edge of the sink, and I could feel them shaking. Finally I gave in and put my hands on her hips, then around the small of her back. "All right," I whispered.

Holding her reminded me of when I was younger, when men and women often met and came together quickly. There was an abandon, a sense of ease and assurance to it that I now realized I missed. Something was happening between us; it was unspoken, yet there was no avoiding or denying it. She moved her face up along my neck until her lips touched my jaw. Then she kissed me deeply, with the familiarity of a long time lover. I held her tighter and our kiss extended into a probing which seemed enhanced by the absolute dark. There was nothing but our mouths and tongues in the black void, and I realized my hands were no longer shaking, but my knees were trembling.

The gentle knock on the door made her body go rigid and she pulled her head away.

"Laura," Paul whispered. His voice was so close. He must have had his mouth right up to the edge of the door. "Laura, I know you're in there."

In the dark her hand came up and covered my mouth. Then she whispered, "Go away, Paul."

"Laura, come out."

"Leave me alone."

At first Paul said nothing. We could hear his breathing. It became more pronounced, more labored, extended inhalations, followed by long quivering sighs. The man was overwrought and finally he released a sob. "You're driving me crazy," he whispered. "I know why you're going to Chicago. What's his name?"

After a moment, Laura said, "Richard." I hadn't told her my name, and her hand must have felt some reaction, some contraction in my face. Her fingers seemed to hold my jaw with even greater intent, yet tenderly. I nodded my head. "His name is Richard," she repeated.

"Please," Paul said, his voice hardly audible, "tell me you won't see Richard."

"At the moment, I can't see anybody." Her thumb and forefinger pressed into the corners of my mouth and gently lifted, forming a smile on my lips.

"Don't make fun of me."

"I won't," she said, as her fingers played over my lips, "if you'll just leave me alone."

"You know I can't," Paul whispered.

"You've never tried," Laura said.

"Let me come to Chicago with you. Whatever you do with Richard, you can do with me."

"It might get crowded," she said.

"Chicago's a big town," Paul said rather hopefully.

"You have a point there." Her fingers hesitated over my lips. I feared that she was about to withdraw them. Slowly I opened my mouth and moved my head forward. First I took just the tip of her forefinger, tasting nail polish. Then I consumed the finger, long and slender, up past the middle knuckle, sucking on it gently. She pressed closer to me.

"You're thinking about it?" Paul said. "What we could do in Chicago?"

"I'm thinking about Chicago, yes."

"We could at least talk there. Really talk."

"We always *really talk*, Paul. That's the last thing I need in Chicago."

"What else could we do there? Tell me."

"It's not something that can be explained, Paul. You don't understand that. You never have. You understand everything else. Politics, history, books you've read, books you haven't read, the Spartans basketball team—*everything*—but you don't understand this." She pushed her finger deeper into my mouth.

"What do you mean *this*?" Paul said, his voice for the first time slightly demanding. "Define *this.*"

"No, Paul," she said, "with you *this* wouldn't be the same."

"And this *Richard* does? He understands *this*? Why?"

"*Why?* Well, this Richard—Richard *is* a trip to Chicago. Dark, close, mysterious. Sort of like this train." She turned her hand slightly and inserted another finger in my mouth. "Richard is

Chicago, and you—Paul, you are East Lansing."

I bit down gently on her fingers.

Beyond the door, Paul began to weep. He sniffled and gurgling sounds came from his throat. "This is crazy," he said. "You're crazy."

"Perhaps," she said. "But how else is there to be?"

Paul took a deep breath. He sounded like he was composing himself. "All right. Fine. Go to Chicago." There was a loud slap, the sound of an open palm hitting the door. *"Go* to Chicago." Then we heard his footsteps as he walked toward the back of the passenger car.

Laura removed her fingers from my mouth.

"How did you know my name?" I asked.

"I don't know, I just did. Isn't that something?"

"Is there a Richard in Chicago?"

She didn't answer. Her body was withdrawing suddenly—though we were still in each others arms, there was in her the clear desire for release. Finally, she said, "I'm worried."

"About what?"

"Paul."

"He did as you asked."

"But he never has before." She reached around me for the door latch. "I must—" she opened the door and stepped out of the lavatory.

•

Standing alone in the dark lavatory I began to understand why I was on the train. When Carolyn and I went to Chicago, we didn't talk or think about policy. We ate and drank in good restaurants and bars, we went to exhibits at the Art Institute, we stayed out in blues clubs until the early morning hours. We made love in hotel rooms, ordered room service, then made love again. We liked to walk the busy sidewalks on Michigan Avenue or in The Loop. There, we weren't bureaucrats, we were like everyone else—like the men, women and children who passed us, who didn't know us, who would never see us again, who would never care about or be affected by the policy decisions we made, and in that sidewalk anonymity there was a sense of union, perhaps even communion, where people tacitly agree to share the same sidewalk on a busy street in a large American city. To conduct ourselves in such an orderly, civic manner seemed a remarkable human achievement. People went home and committed the most heinous crimes and indignities against one another, but out on the streets of Chicago we behaved. I remember one moment in particular: we were standing in a group of a dozen or so pedestrians, waiting patiently for the light to change. It was November and steam rose from manhole covers and an icy wind blew in from Lake Michigan. Despite the cold we waited, together. A seven- or eight-year-old black girl was standing next to me, holding her mother's hand. She had colored beads in her hair that clicked together in the breeze. When the traffic light changed she looked up at me with lovely, sincere eyes and said, "We can go now." It was not obedience that caused us to all cross the street only when the light changed, and it was not simply a matter of safety; it was more an urgency, a desire to belong—not to stand out, not to lead, and certainly not to be recognized—but simply to belong. I don't understand why this is so appealing; I only know that I felt it, Carolyn felt it, and that we only felt it in Chicago.

For some reason I thought Laura would understand all this. I pulled on my coat and followed her. The passenger car was not pitch black like the lavatory. A faint glow was cast through the windows by the snow. Laura had almost reached the back of the car. She turned and looked toward me once, then opened the rear door and went outside.

I went down the aisle but stopped where the old woman sat. She looked up at me and said, "It reminds me of those glass globes children love. Where you shake the globe and the snow swirls around the beautiful scene."

"Yes, it does," I said.

I continued down the aisle, walking sideways, excusing myself as I brushed by seated passengers. When I reached the back door, I pulled it open and stepped out into driving snow. I hesitated a moment. The snow was remarkably heavy. An absolute white-out. I could see nothing to either side of the train except white. I tried the door to the next car, but it was locked. Turning to my right I climbed down the steps. The snow was deep, halfway to my knees at least. There was something dark lying in the snow. Leaning down I saw that it was Laura's water bottle.

I walked out a ways from the train, perhaps five yards. Even at that distance the train was difficult to see, and all around me there was nothing but the snow. I continued to walk farther from the train. The land inclined gradually—a field, I suspected. Finally I stopped and turned slowly so that I could see in all directions. There was nothing but the snow, and the gray line of the train.

I turned up my coat collar and put on my gloves. My hands weren't shaking. In fact, despite the gusting wind, I was not uncomfortable. The cold air felt good on my face, in my sinuses. It was as though I hadn't been able to breathe for a long time, and I could take long deep drafts of air way down into my lungs.

I continued to walk out into the field, and finally I called Laura's name. After several minutes I called Paul's name. Each time I'd yell a name I'd pause to see if there was a response, but there was only the sound of the wind. I stopped and looked all around again. If possible, the blizzard seemed to be getting worse.

Suddenly the lights came on in the train, and the engine started up. I had walked farther away from the tracks then I had thought, and it surprised me that I was so high above the train.

I began walking down the hill. As the engine's pitch revved higher and higher, I began to run, which was difficult with the depth of the snow. Some drifts were up to my thighs. I was perhaps twenty yards from the train when it began to move. I called out, though I couldn't even hear myself over the noise of the engine and wind. I kept wading through the snow, but the train was picking up speed. When the second to last car, the one I'd been on, passed by I was only a few feet from the tracks. The train moved slowly but steadily; there was something relentless and determined in the way it rolled on into the blizzard. I could see the passengers clearly, and I saw Paul and Laura, leaning on the counter of the concession stand, being waited on by the young black man in the white coat. They stood close together, sipping from styrofoam cups, and they didn't appear concerned that I wasn't on the train. No one seemed to notice that I was missing.

As the passenger car continued by I saw the old woman, still in her seat, gazing out into the night. I waved my arms and called out, despite the sound of the train. Her head was propped on her hand and she appeared content that the train was moving again. She didn't see me; she didn't respond, but only continued to stare out into the night.

Then the train was gone, a gray streak that faded into the whiteness, its sound disappearing into the wind. I stepped onto the tracks, where the snow wasn't very deep. I couldn't remember how close I was to the last town the train had passed through. I looked west; then I looked east. Then I looked west again.

The Meetinghouse

Hannah LeClaire climbed the steep path, rehearsing her lines. She was nineteen, her legs were strong again, and she liked to walk, even on such overcast Cape Cod afternoons, when the east wind could make April seem colder than January. Below her lay the salt marsh and, in the distance, the shoals off Nauset Beach. When she reached the top of the bluff she turned away from the water and crossed the clearing to the Meetinghouse, a small white clapboard building with black shutters, double front doors and a low steeple. Its simplicity was always the first thing that struck her.

The front doors were unlocked and she let herself inside. Pale light from the tiny windows barely illuminated the rows of deeply scarred and worn benches. "For generations," she recited from memory, as she walked up the center aisle, "people from all over the world have traveled to the Meetinghouse because it represents a unique combination of community and individualism, conformity and rebellion, faith in common humanity and belief in a higher entity. Ralph Waldo Emerson and Walt Whitman both spoke here. Winston Churchill said that he was 'Honored to sit in the handsome, simple house that only American democracy could build.' Mahatma Gandhi referred to it as America's Taj Mahal."

Hannah reached the front of the room, where there was a small riser and, to the left, a simple pulpit. She stepped up to the pulpit and turned to face the rows of benches. She imagined them filled with tourists. They would be wearing shorts and T-shirts. She would be wearing traditional Colonial dress. Theresa Cluff, who had been a guide last year, said that by August she would come to dread the weight of that dress, the smell of wool in summer heat and humidity. Even worse was the predictability of the tourists. They often asked you to pose for photographs. Small children would become restless; babies would wail and scream. After a while, Theresa said, you swear they're the same people every day, from places like Iowa and Kentucky. It would be hard to remember that for most of them this would be their one visit to the Meetinghouse. What you never get used to, Theresa said, is how often people come and weep.

Hannah stepped to the side of the pulpit and suddenly did a little soft shoe, concluding with a double stomp of her feet, with outstretched arms. That would lighten them up. She laughed, and her voice echoed off the rafters—then it was suddenly accompanied by clapping. Hannah stepped backwards, her hip striking the pulpit.

In the darkness at the back of the room, she saw movement—a pair of hands, then the slightest gleam: the roundness of a man's shaved head. Not bald, she was certain: shaved.

"You're absolutely right," he said, his voice resonating deeply. "It's all just Vaudeville now. And merchandise: souvenirs and baseball caps." He stepped forward—he was tall and lean—and walked to the nearest window and looked out. His skull was perfectly smooth, but his trim moustache seemed to give his head definition. He might have been ten years older than she was and something about his manner, the way he kept his hands in his coat pockets, suggested that he was not dangerous.

"By June they'll be coming down to the Cape by the busload." He turned his head toward her. His eyes were pale blue, catching the light from the window. He was wearing a good overcoat. Dark wool, knee-length; the collar was turned up. "That spiel you'll be giving them, do you believe it?"

"It's true," she said.

"That's not what I asked."

"The historical society researched it carefully."

"I'm not talking about names and dates," he said.

She wondered if he might be a teacher. He had a way of directing the discussion which reminded her of the few good teachers she'd had—somehow they always managed to get you to a predetermined conclusion, as though you had known the answer all along. "You mean what the Meetinghouse symbolizes?"

"Yes," he said. "You believe that?"

"Well, sure. I suppose, however—I suppose things have changed. America, I mean. I suppose we've lost connection with what this place *really* means. People say it all the time: we've lost something. But no one really knows how or why. It's sad. A lot of people cry when they come here."

"Yes, it is—sad." He stared at her for a moment. It made her uncomfortable. "Still, it must be an honor to be selected to be a guide at the Meetinghouse."

"When I was eight I had a neighbor who was a guide. I've looked forward to it ever since."

He seemed to be smiling beneath that moustache, but there was something in those pale eyes—she couldn't really tell from this distance, in such poor light. Then, very simply, as though she weren't even present, he walked to the double doors and let himself out.

Hannah suddenly felt weak and she sat on the first bench. Her heart was beating fast, and for a moment she could only stare at a knot in the floorboard. Then, looking up, she watched as the man passed by the windows along the left side of the building. She went out the side door and looked across the gravel parking lot behind the Meetinghouse. He was climbing into a gray car, something old but well maintained, something European. He rolled down the window and said, "A lift to the village?"

She hesitated.

"Perhaps not," he said.

She walked across the gravel and climbed in. The car had bucket seats, black leather that smelled rich and creaked whenever she moved. When he turned on the ignition, the engine rumbled deeply. She was afraid to look at him, so she watched his hands. The knob on the stick shift looked like it was made of ivory.

"What is this? It looks like it belongs in an old black and white movie."

"It's a Mercedes," he said, putting the car in gear. "I suppose it is an old black and white movie."

She watched his left foot and his right hand as he shifted through the gears. Halfway down the hill, he pulled up on the wide, sandy shoulder that overlooked the marsh. "Ever drive a standard?"

She wanted to lie, but for some reason the question seemed incredibly personal. She shook her head.

"Care to learn?"

She stared out her window. The tide was high and the inlets knotting the marsh were flooded.

"Not here on the hill," he said. "The parking lot at the beach, that would be perfect. No traffic, no hills, no turns."

She looked at him then. He was so pale and up close his skull was covered with a fine black stubble. She was reminded of her armpits after shaving. His eyes were direct, yet acquiescent. "Are you thirty?" she asked.

He smiled. "Not quite. But I'm old enough to give a driving lesson."

"I should get home. It'll be dark soon."

"All right. Perhaps another time."

"Perhaps."

•

His name was Martin Kline and he was a doctoral student at Brandeis University. He was on the Cape doing research on the Meetinghouse for his dissertation. Late afternoons he waited for her in his car by the rotary in Chatham, and he always had cold bottles of Coke. They would drive up to Nauset Beach in Orleans, where the parking lot was long and empty. Hannah would sit in the driver's seat, working the gears, and, despite being so nervous she could feel the sweat running beneath her clothes, she couldn't believe how splendid shifting felt. She only ground the gears occasionally; he was very patient, even when she stalled out.

After several sessions she wasn't thinking about it all the time—it had become part of driving. In fact, she had noticed when driving her mother's car, a Chevrolet with automatic transmission, that she missed shifting, and often would depress an imaginary clutch with her left foot.

"Let's go somewhere," she said on yet another overcast afternoon. "I can't drive around the parking lot forever."

"Think you're ready?" he asked, and she nodded. "Well, it's not like there's a lot of traffic on the Cape this time of year. All right, head toward Chatham Light."

She never got out of third gear, the road was so windy. Downshifting to second as she came out of curves was particularly good; the engine surged and the car accelerated toward the next bend. Below the lighthouse there was a cluster of summer cottages, mostly closed for the winter.

"Why don't you pull into this one up on the left," Martin said. When they had stopped in the drive, he opened his door. "Come on in for a minute. I've got Cokes, then we'll get you back to the village."

"You live here?"

"Belongs to my aunt, and I'm staying here while I do my research. Come on—I want to show you something." He walked away, and after a moment she got out of the car.

The cottage was small. Weathered shingles and white trim that was peeling badly. Inside there was a sliding glass door with a clear view across Pleasant Bay to North Beach and the Monomoy Cut-Through. He was using the dining room table as an office. Stacks of books and papers surrounded a computer. He got her a Coke from the refrigerator, a bottle of beer for himself.

"I want to ask you a favor," he said, leaning against the kitchen counter. A large gray cat sat at the edge of the sink and he stroked the back of its head. "I have to go up to Boston for a while and I was wondering if you'd check on the place for me. Gracie will need food and water, and I know she'd like the company. I understand that these summer places can get vandalized, and I'd rather not have to pack everything up."

"When will you be back?"

"Ten, twelve days."

She sipped her Coke and stared out the sliding glass door.

"I could pay you fifty dollars."

"That's not necessary."

"It'd only be fair."

She walked into the living room, where one wall was lined with pine shelves full of old books, which gave off a musty odor that made her feel as though she might sneeze. "This place is a black and white movie, too," she said.

•

Her mother was a nurse at the hospital in Hyannis and she often worked the evening shift. Most afternoons Hannah walked from the high school, up through the village, and out to the cottage. Though it was several miles, she liked the walk. Occasionally boys from school would slow down in their cars and offer her a ride, but she turned them down. The cottage was her secret; walking there, Hannah imaged she was someone else, someone— an adult—with a mysterious past, not a high school senior. She should have graduated the year before, so her classmates this year pretty much left her alone. Some boys, however, watched her, looking for encouragement. They knew about her, and their eyes were often crude. At the cottage Gracie would climb in her lap if she sat in the leather reading chair. Gracie liked to be stroked behind the ears. She would purr as her claws worked into Hannah's skirt, sometimes hooking into her thighs.

A draft of Martin's dissertation was in a box on the dining room table, and on the second visit Hannah took it to the leather chair and began reading. She knew she should have permission to do so, but she couldn't resist. It wasn't as though it were his diary. She skimmed the portions of the dissertation that were filled with statistics. However, once she got to the actual history of the Meetinghouse she felt like she was reading a story. The present structure was actually the second meetinghouse to be built on the bluff overlooking the bay. The first had been built in 1698 by a group of disenchanted parishoners from Harwich, after having had differences with the minister of the parish. Eventually several families moved out of the village to the other side of the bay, where they wanted to establish a new parish. This outraged those loyal to the old parish and its minister, Reverend Wentworth. One night in April, just as the new meetinghouse was nearly completed, a group of men from the first parish quietly dismantled the building and hauled the timbers off in boats. When the new parishoners found their Meetinghouse had vanished, some believed it to be an act of God. Others went to confront the old parishoners. Throughout the following summer there were a number of skirmishes around the bay. Fistfights. Boats burned. Fish weirs and lobster traps cut. A man named Leander Clarke lost an eye from birdshot fired from a blunderbuss. Lumber that had been taken from the meetinghouse was said to have been used in the building of houses, barns and boats from Provincetown to Nantucket. Finally, after much bad feeling between families—often, even, within families—Reverend Wentworth granted the breakaway parishoners the right to build a new meetinghouse, and to seek the services of another minister. They found a young man, Caleb Lowell, who came down from Cambridge. Martin's dissertation stopped there, which was frustrating because it was suggested that after a few seasons Reverend Lowell ran into great difficulties with his parishoners over a woman.

•

On Saturday Hannah went to the Meetinghouse for what was called orientation. The girls practiced reciting their tour guide speeches for the older women on the committee. Mrs. Colby was there, but Hannah kept her distance. Hannah had her speech down cold, unlike some of the other girls. Later they tried on the traditional clothes. Theresa Cluff had been right: the wool skirts and cape were heavy, and the bonnets were just plain dumb. When Mrs. Doyle noted that Hannah's blouse would have to be let out,

Janice Sloane made a comment that caused several girls to laugh. Hannah ignored them.

Afterwards she walked out to the cottage. It was sunny, one of the first warm days of the year, and when she arrived she looked in the refrigerator and found that there were no more Cokes. She opened one of the beers. It had been over a year, and she drank this beer down fast as she watched Gracie eat. She opened another beer and took it out on the small deck beyond the sliding glass door. She stood in the sunlight and warm air, without wearing her winter coat —standing outside without that coat on was something she hadn't done in months—and for a while she felt splendid, as splendid as those first afternoons when she had shifted through the gears of Martin's Mercedes. Soon after finishing the beer, however, she became drowsy, and she went into the bedroom, lay down on her back, and fell asleep to the rhythm of Gracie's purring in her left ear.

•

She dreamed again that her feet were painfully trapped in the stirrups just before she awoke with a start. She was aware of Gracie's absence; then, turning her head, she saw Martin standing in the doorway. He was wearing sunglasses. She started to get up, but then realized that she was soaked with sweat and was chilled.

"Stay put," he said quietly. He took the blanket from the rocking chair, came to the bed and spread it over her. "You were having a nightmare, I guess."

She wiped her forehead and closed her eyes. "I had to leave school last year." Her voice was shaking and she was afraid that she would start to cry. "God, why can't I get *past* this?"

"You will." He took off his sunglasses. His eyes were different. There was something in them that she had not seen before. They weren't crude, but there was a longing, and she could see that he was embarrassed by it. "How about if I made you some tea?" But he didn't move.

She took her arm out from beneath the blanket and reached for his hand. He held it tightly, then knelt on the floor and laid his head on her lap. She ran her other hand over his scalp as she sobbed.

•

They slept, both fully clothed; he remained outside the blanket. Gracie was curled up between their knees. When Hannah awoke she could smell low tide.

"Feeling better?" he whispered.

"At least I didn't have any nightmares," she said.

"You want to tell me about them?"

"No."

"Okay," he said.

"I want you to tell me about Reverend Lowell and the woman."

"I hoped you'd read my dissertation," he said. "I've been involved in it for so many years now. The reverend and the woman. Old story. He was young. She was younger."

"What was her name?"

"Mercy Compton. How's that for a New Englander's name? She was about fifteen. One account says she had long black hair and the greenest eyes, and a figure that—despite the cut of Puritan dresses—would bring silence when she entered a room. *Very* disturbing to the elders, I'm sure."

"They didn't sew a scarlet letter on her or anything?"

"No. She removed to Rhode Island. I've lost track of her after that."

"And Reverend Lowell lost his ministry?"

"You could say that." Martin paused until she turned her head on the pillow. His eyes were so direct and blue. "Hung himself, from a rafter in the Meetinghouse, actually."

"That's not in our tour guide speeches."

"While you were sleeping, you said—" He touched her face with his warm hand. "What happened to the boy?"

"Enlisted in the navy. There were complications. I can't have children."

•

By the end of April driving the Mercedes was second nature. One afternoon they were on Route 28—even with the windows opened they could still smell the fried clams they'd eaten in the car at a place in Orleans.

"I don't get these road signs," Martin said. "Here we are, going south along Pleasant Bay and that sign says we're on 28 North."

"Cape Cod logic."

"Logic? Right now we're heading south, and if you take this road through Chatham and around the elbow, you're then heading west—but the signs still say 28 North. Driving in this direction this road *never* goes north."

"Cape Cod is a crooked arm, right? So one minute you're going one way; five miles later you're going another. So they figure the bridges at the Canal as the top of the Cape, and you travel down from there. Through Barnstable and the Upper Cape at the bicep, around the elbow, then up the forearm—the Lower Cape—to Provincetown. It's not a compass thing."

"It's not a compass thing," he mimicked, and they both laughed.

Then, as they rounded the bend in the road, Hannah downshifted expertly, as the patrol car came into view, parked on the side of the road amidst a stand of scrub oaks. Hannah took the next curve, but soon the cruiser appeared in the rear-view mirror, gaining quickly, lights flashing. The sight caused a constriction in her chest, and she felt her face heat up. She pulled off the road into the sand and watched the cruiser stop behind them. As she expected, it was Sergeant Colby who got out of the cruiser. She glanced at Martin, who appeared calm as he dug the car registration out of the glove compartment. When he looked at her, his mouth turned grim, as though he had seen something unexpected in her face.

Sergeant Colby leaned down to her window, pushing his reflector sunglasses back against the bridge of his nose. His face was wide and blunt, and his shave was so close that his cheeks had a faint sheen. "Hannah, this isn't your car." Then, reaching across for the registration, he said to Martin, "Of course not. And you are—her uncle?"

"I'm sorry," she said, removing her license from her wallet and holding it up to Colby, "I might have taken that corner too fast."

"You've lived here all your life," Colby said. "You should know Route 28 doesn't get any straighter because you're driving a Mercedes Benz." He glanced at the registration a moment. "Mr. Kline of Boston, you're down here on vacation a bit early."

"I'm living here temporarily."

"Why would you want to do that, for the fried seafood?" Colby sniffed and almost smiled.

"I'm conducting research." Colby seemed unimpressed. "On the Meetinghouse."

"Uh-huh. Living temporarily where?"

"My aunt's—Jane Kendall's—down White's Lane."

"Mr. Kline, you always let teenage girls drive your car like this?" He took the license from Hannah's fingers and walked back to his cruiser.

"The 'uncle' bit was a nice touch," Martin said.

She looked at Martin then, and he took her hand—only because his was so steady did she realize that she was trembling. They sat without talking for several minutes, then she put both hands on the wheel as Sergeant Colby approached the car again.

"I'm only giving you a warning," Sergeant Colby said, handing her the slip. Speaking across to Martin, he said, "I'd suggest, mister, that you be careful about who drives this car."

•

Her mother left Friday morning to attend a nurses' conference in Hartford. After school Hannah went home and packed one small suitcase. Her mother had taken tomato sauce out of the freezer, and Hannah packed that as well. About nine o'clock, when it was dark, the Mercedes pulled up in front of the house.

Martin helped her put the suitcase in the backseat, then said,

"You know, we could go somewhere for the weekend. Up to New Hampshire or Maine. Or maybe to Boston?"

"You mean 'remove'—isn't that the word you use in your dissertation?" She put her hand on his as it rested on the gear shift.

"No, you've got work to do, and I have another orientation meeting. Besides, I've brought my mother's killer tomato sauce."

"The tomato, in Mercy Compton's day, was the devil's food." Martin lowered his voice and whispered, "It was believed to incite the passions."

"So why go away, when we have the sauce right here?"

"Precisely." Though it was dark, he was wearing his sunglasses. He wore them often since she had said they made him look cool. He put the Mercedes in gear and shook his head. "The thought of you staying with me till Sunday is—it's been driving me nuts all week."

"Me too."

"Because you have a figure," he intoned in a deep voice, "that can bring silence to a roomful of elders."

She laughed, then put her arm around his shoulders and kissed his neck.

"We'll be able to have breakfast together," he said. "How do you like your eggs?"

"In bed."

•

In bed Hannah found herself telling Martin about herself and the boy. How since eighth grade, when she'd begun to develop hips and breasts, boys had paid attention to her. They looked at her eagerly, and she knew that her body was a source of jokes, of remarks. Girls also took notice. In the shower after gym class sometimes girls would glance at her as though in awe. They'd make jokes too, but more often, particularly once they'd gotten into high school, they'd warn her to keep away from the boys they liked. Even male teachers treated her differently. They tended to touch her on the shoulder when passing out papers, and often when she looked up from her desk she'd see them avert their eyes quickly.

The boy's name was Jack Colby. He was a senior the year she was a junior. Jack played soccer and hung out with the coolest group of guys in his class. Hannah couldn't believe his legs, how they controlled the soccerball, how he baffled his opponents with his footwork. He asked her out, and quickly she found herself in a crowd of kids who seemed to drink and smoke dope all the time. The following summer, when she discovered she was pregnant, she actually thought that it was a good thing. She imagined herself quitting school—which she had come to dislike intensely—and going off to college with her husband. Colleges and universities had family housing, and she imagined living there, raising the baby while Jack studied something like marketing or pre-law—not criminal justice, because he had made it clear he had no interest ending up a small town cop like his father. When she told Jack her period was late, he was stunned, but he said something like that could be worked out. That's what he said, *We could work it out.* But once she was certain that she was pregnant she wouldn't see him for days, and when she did he was distant, nervous, even frightened. Finally, he told her his parents were furious, and his father had decided that Jack needed to get straightened out.

"So he joined the service," Martin said.

"He's in the Meditteranean."

"Your mother, what did she do?"

"She arranged to have it taken care of. Jack's parents paid for it. Last time I saw Sergeant Colby before the other day he and his wife were sitting at our kitchen table and he was writing a check to my mother. There were complications, and I missed so much school I had to repeat this year."

Martin was staring at the ceiling, with Gracie perched on his bare chest. The room was lit only by candles and long shadows danced on the walls. "You've been ostracized by your community."

"They hardly speak to me, except for some boy who wants to

get his hands on me. Some of them tape anonymous notes with drawings to my locker. Teachers treat me like I was a—a pariah. At least Mercy Compton got to *remove* to Rhode Island."

She had been sitting up against the headboard and Martin turned and looked at her. "When you graduate, you would like to do that—leave the Cape?" She nodded. "Have you made any plans? Applied to college?"

"UMass. I'm not even sure my mother can afford that."

"What happened to your father?"

"Haven't heard from him since I was four. Mom just says he found a job overseas."

"You want to do that, go to college?"

She laid down next to him. "I don't know. I just know I don't want to end up like my mother—tired and raising a kid on my own. That's why I agreed to it."

•

Saturday afternoon Hannah and the other guides were to go to the Meetinghouse to get their altered costumes and pose for the annual group photograph. This was a favorite part of the tradition, and the framed photographs from previous years were hung on the back wall of the Meetinghouse. Martin offered to drive her.

"No, I'll walk. I always do."

"It's a good ways from down here."

"It's a good day for it," she said as she pulled on her coat. "Besides, from here I could walk most of the way along the beach."

"Then I'll walk with you. Part way, at least—until my legs give out. Then I'll hobble back here and get some work done."

They went down through the dunes and headed north along the beach. The bay was flat and there was only the slightest east wind. Occasionally Martin tried to skim a stone, but he wasn't very good at it. There was something uneasy between them and they didn't speak until they were around the southern point of Tuppin Cove. "What is it," he said finally, "you're embarrassed to have them see me with you?"

She kept walking, staring down at the smooth, wet sand. "Actually, I thought it would be difficult for you being seen with me."

"God, Hannah—"

"It's all right if we're in your car. Or in the cottage. Some *place* where we're concealed, where it's just the two of us. But everywhere we'd go people would make these, these as*sump*tions. People say they don't care, that these things don't matter anymore, but they do—they *do* take notice."

"Notice of what?" he said angrily.

"They'd see you as a man who's screwing this teenage girl."

"What does it matter that *they* notice?"

"But it *does*—can you understand that?"

Martin threw his stone—it skipped twice on the water—then he kept walking, as though he hadn't heard, as though he didn't want to hear. Hannah stopped, and waited until he turned around and came back to her.

"Where are we going?" he said. "That's what you're really asking. Where is this going?"

"You're going to finish your research and return to Boston," she said.

"And you'll graduate high school, and then what?" He stood straight and narrow with his hands in his coat pockets, his collar turned up. "Then what, Hannah?"

She looked out at the water. The breeze was stronger now that they'd rounded the point, and cold tears formed at the corners of her eyes.

"Listen," he said, "Let me give you a piece of my own history. When I was in my early twenties, I was married for less than a year. It was a mistake—we were both too young. But you and I are different. This has nothing to do with age, and you know it. You could come back to Boston with me," he said, stepping closer. "Graduate this spring, then—"

"I'm going to guide this summer. Told you, I've wanted to since I was eight years old."

"All right then, guide. I'll be coming down to the Cape often this summer anyway. But we could plan for next fall. Get you enrolled in college—"

She glared at him then, her tears running down her cold cheeks. He looked rebuked—he might have been a boy who had been told that his fantastic plans were just too silly. Then she walked on quickly, her feet smacking on the hard sand. Raising her head, she shouted up into the wind, *"Uncle!"*

•

She was late when she reached the Meetinghouse and the other girls were already dressed in their costumes. When they and the mothers and grandmothers who fussed about their garments turned to Hannah there was something new in their eyes—not direct accusation, which she had seen so often, but a shy, uncertain glance before looking away.

Mrs. Colby stood by the open front doors of the Meetinghouse, talking to the photographer, a heavy man with several cameras hanging around his neck. She kept a thin shoulder toward Hannah, and raising a cigarette to her mouth her cheek went hollow as she inhaled fiercely. Menthols: winter nights Jack would park his mother's Ford by Webster's cranberry bog, where he knew the police never checked, turn the heater up, and Hannah could smell mentholated tobacco while they made love. The thought of menthol now made her nauseous.

It was Althea Sloane who approached Hannah. "Dear, we thought that perhaps you had decided not to participate." She placed a frail hand on Hannah's wrist and cocked her head. "Are you feeling all right? I wonder if you shouldn't be home in bed, you're so pale."

"I've been cut. Right?"

Althea, who was well into her seventies, had a perpetual nod, a symptom of Parkinson's, so she always appeared to be in agreement. "Well, the board members did have to make some difficult decisions last night."

"But I was chosen."

"Yes, you were, dear—but you're really from last year's class, and of course you took ill and, you see, there are so many new girls eligible this year—"

Turning away from the old woman, Hannah bumped into Michelle Calder, causing her bonnet to tip forward and cover her eyes. Hannah strode across the clearing, then ran down the bluff path to the beach.

•

She only walked several hundred yards along the beach before she stopped because she was crying so hard her ribcage ached with each gulp of air. Down near the waterline there was an abandoned dory stuck in the sand; she climbed in and sat on the thwart facing the bow. Even after she stopped crying, after she caught her breath, she remained in the dory. The tide was coming in and the water was creeping up the beach toward the rotted hull. When the sun set, the clouds out over the bay turned rose and purple, deepening by the minute. Occasionally seagulls landed nearby and observed her in silence.

There was a stiff piece of rope, caked with sand, salt and dried kelp, still attached to the bow cleat; she untied it, coiled it at her feet. Then she tried to make a noose at one end, but it didn't come out right, so she made a knot she was sure of, two half-hitches.

•

Because the wind was out of the southeast, bringing rain clouds in off the ocean at dusk, Hannah didn't hear the footsteps behind her until they had almost reached the dory. She turned and looked up at Martin. He was wearing a hat, an old fisherman's cap with a long shiny black bill.

"Permission to come aboard?"

"Granted."

He sat on the bow thwart, facing her. "I drove up to the Meetinghouse," he said. "Everyone was gone. I watched you from the bluff for I don't know how long. You sat here preoccupied with something, your hands and arms working, but I couldn't tell what from that distance."

"Jack's mother got them to cut me from the guides."

"I gathered that."

Hannah held out the rope. Martin didn't take it, but kept his hands stuffed in his coat pockets. "This is the best I could come up with," she said.

"Looks like it would do the job."

"If they found a local girl hanging from the rafters, it would probably boost tourism."

"No doubt," he said.

"You'd have to rewrite your history."

"Could require a whole new chapter."

"What would it say?"

"I suppose it could be connected to Mercy Compton and Reverend Lowell, but certain opposites would have to be taken into consideration. Opposites that seem appropriate to our time. She dies, then he leaves the Cape and disappears. And of course he's no minister from Cambridge."

"Is there a point?"

He looked down at the rope in her hands. "Is there a point to any piece of history? I suppose we write it to find out what the point is." He raised his eyes, and looked past her, toward the Meetinghouse on the bluff. Hannah didn't turn around, and she could feel the first drops of rain on her face. "I suspect," he said, "the point is that the Meetinghouse will still be there after all of us are gone, regardless of how we live our lives, what we do with them. It'll still be up there on that hill overlooking the bay."

"Tourists will continue to come."

"Definitely."

"Some will cry," she said.

"I hope so."

"Perhaps that's the point?"

He looked cold; his cheeks were flushed, and she wasn't used to seeing such color in his face. Nor had she ever seen him in a hat. He stared at her then. The tan canvas of his hat darkened with the rain. "I would," he said.

Standing, she dropped the knotted end of the rope in the bottom of the dory. He got up, too, and they climbed over the gunwale and started back toward the bluff. A steady rain was now at their backs, and the wind seemed to push them along the shoreline. They kept their heads down, staring only at the firm sand in front of each step, never once looking up toward their destination.

Absolution

I

Bless me, Father, for I have sinned. It has been more than one week since my last confession. In fact, it's been a long time— months—since my last confession. These are my sins: I said bad words; I had dirty thoughts; I did dirty deeds. These have been my sins since I turned twelve; they're a part of me, I guess, as much as my legs, my arms, my ability to breathe. Now there's something else and I'm not sure what to call it.

I'm a junior at Boston College. These guys from St. John's Seminary come over to our dorm, and one of them, Jerome, grew up with me in Dedham. Usually we sit around my room drinking, smoking cigarettes, listening to the stereo, talking about stuff. Lately we've been talking about temptation of the flesh; it has led to a situation that I need to confess, and not just in the ordinary way. I need to explain it carefully, so please have patience with me.

I suspect that Jerome will be a good priest someday, but he's having his doubts right now. Just about every BC guy can drink, but these guys who come over from the seminary, they're something else. The joke is: Look what they have to look forward to. Jerome can drink anyone under the table, doesn't show it, except that sometimes he breaks out into Latin. I was an altarboy and learned my Latin responses, but it's like he's speaking in tongues.

Jerome and I have been neighbors since parochial school. After ninth grade, I went to Dedham High and Jerome went over to St. Sebastian's. It was obvious even then that he was going to take "the call." Jerome was a good basketball player at St. Sibbies, and someday he hopes to coach boys basketball, but only after he goes off and does missionary work in another country. I can see him, living in some South American village, helping them dig wells and build better houses. He wants to be that kind of a priest.

Sometimes, when we're drinking in the dorms, we play a game we call Confession. It's like this: one of us begins to confess made-up sins, and when it's done the other delivers penance. Now since I gave my first real confession, I've almost always gotten the same penance. I'm not trying to persuade you, Father, but it's a fact. It's always been three Hail Marys, three Our Fathers, and an Act of Contrition. The worst I've ever gotten—and it was just once, when I was in high school—is five Hail Marys, five Our Fathers, and three Acts of Contrition, and there wasn't anything particularly different that I confessed that time. The usual suspects, if you know what I mean. The priest wasn't from our parish, and I think that had something to do with it. He was this drifter priest; he came to our church occasionally and filled in for a week or so, and he was famous for these really tough sermons. It was like he was angry all the time, and I wouldn't be surprised if it had something to do with his not having his own parish.

I don't think Jerome will ever be that kind of priest, no matter how much he travels. When we play Confession, he goes pretty light. And sometimes I'll really try to get him to nail me. Remember, this is a game, and we're drinking, and believe me by midnight in the dorms it's like a riot's going on. I mean guys are bowling in the halls—with a full set of candlepins—or they're playing hall hockey. You might have even seen that news spot on WBZ a while back—college kids in nothing but their underwear doing swan dives out the third floor window into the snowbanks? That was my dorm.

Then, of course, there's girls. We have parietal hours on Friday and Saturday in the dorms, but guys sneak girls in so they don't have to check them out at the lobby desk by eleven. Sometimes

in the middle of the night you can hear a girl's voice from another room. Or you go down to the lav Sunday morning and a
football player is standing outside the door, saying, Wait until
she's done. So you stand out in the hall until the girl comes out
in a big bathrobe, and he hustles her back to his room.

It was when we were playing Confession that I got this idea
about Jerome. One night we were pretty ripped and Jerome gives
us this confession about sins of the flesh. There was me and my
roommate Neil, and this other seminarian, who had already passed
out. Jerome starts to confess about lusting after a Spanish teacher
he had a couple of years ago when he went to summer school at
Newton South. He described himself and this young teacher—
in her mid-twenties—going at it in the language lab with the
lights out. They both had their headphones on and they were
listening to a Spanish lesson the whole time.

When Jerome finished, Neil said, You mean you didn't take
Latin in high school? And I said, Of course he did, but he also
took Spanish because he knew that one day he was going to do
missionary work in South America—which got us to rolling
around on the floor and the beds laughing so hard it hurt. Then
Neil said that Jerome's confession made him so horny he had to
go see his girlfriend—she's at school over at BU—so he heads
down Comm Ave for a visit.

After Neil left I asked Jerome if he'd ever—I don't know how to
put this—if he'd ever had any experience. You know, with girls.
Jerome's not a bad looking guy, I suppose. Blond, clean cut; no
sideburns, moustache or anything. Wears chinos and blue or
white shirts most of the time, and I can imagine some girl thinking he was *nice* or something. He's evasive, so I ask him about St.
Sibbies—I mean, even Catholic high schools allow for a social
life. Didn't he ever go to dances? Parties? Any dates?

We're sitting on the floor by now, our backs against opposite
bedframes, and the room's only lit by this candle Lucy made for
us—she rooms with Neil's girlfriend. It's huge, weighs about
four pounds and is decorated with peace symbols. I think she
majors in candlemaking at BU; it's that kind of school. Jerome's

looking at me with this little smile, and he's nodding—not saying yes, particularly, but saying, I'm not surprised you're asking me this. If he makes it, Father, he's going to be a good priest, and when people come to talk to him about personal matters—I mean really talk, not just confess to the usual weekly offenses—that smile and nod of his are going to bring a great deal of comfort.

Then Jerome said, You want to know if I'm a virgin?

And I said, Yeah, I guess that's what I'm asking. It's not really a question of being a virgin, Jerome, it's whether you *want* to always be one.

At that moment, I think Jerome and I kind of reversed roles. I mean, among other things, Jerome is being trained to listen to people, to allow them to reveal themselves in a way that will be cleansing. But at that moment I realized that Jerome wanted to confess—I mean, *really* confess—to me.

He started out with a question. Are you one—a virgin? he asked.

And I said, No.

Which is true, I have to tell you. I told him that I certainly wasn't the most experienced twenty-year-old, but no I wasn't a virgin anymore.

Jerome asked, How many?

How many girls? I said. Two.

Then Jerome said, I admit to being curious—no, that's not it either. There are times when I feel *tremendous* temptation.

Jerome, I said, I don't know how you can *avoid* feeling tremendous temptation.

It's not easy, he said. It's very difficult because you don't even know what you're missing.

I asked, Would it be easier, do you think, if you knew?

Then he said something in Latin, and started talking about Orthodox Christianity and how some priests actually used to advocate giving in to temptation, then doing penance and cleansing yourself. It was the only way to rid yourself of sin.

So I asked, What would you do if you had the opportunity, if a woman were willing?

I don't know, Jerome said. After a moment, he added, That's just what I've been asking myself.

This is what I do. Lucy—the candlemaker—if you saw her, you'd probably think, Oh, one of those hippies. She wears long skirts and Indian tops, and if there's a war protest somewhere in Boston, she's there. She always has beads around her neck, and flowers in her long hair. There's this bracelet on her wrist with the name of a soldier in Nam on it—she writes letters to him every week, even though she's never met him. The thing about Lucy is that she is *genuinely* generous. She has these wonderful attributes, Father.

Later in the week Neil and I were down at BU and we took Marie and Lucy out for pizza. Lucy's not my girlfriend or anything, but when we're together with Neil and Marie you might think we are. She sits close to you in a booth, she touches you while she talks, she laughs at what you say. She'll tell a really dirty joke, then the next minute she's weeping over Vietnam. While we were walking back to the girls' apartment, which is just off The Fens, I told her about Jerome. Lucy understood immediately and said, A virgin, when can I meet him?

I said, Keep in mind that he's uncertain. I don't want him to be forced into anything he doesn't, you know, want to do.

Lucy smiled—she has this wonderful smile—and she said, I love taking boys down a rite of passage.

So the following weekend I arranged for Jerome and Lucy to come over to my dorm room. I told Jerome that Lucy's just a friend—she wasn't my girlfriend or anything—and I needed him to help me smuggle her in. My room is on the first floor, which means that Lucy needed a boost to get up on the window sill. Jerome climbed out the window and gave her ten fingers. When we're all back in the room we opened a few beers. And they hit it off immediately. Know what they talked about? Missionary work. About going to other countries and living with people—you'd think they were both ready to sign up for the Peace Corps. The whole time I was just sitting there with my beer, nodding, while he said, then she said, then he said, and so on. Eventually, I got out of there, to go check the fish—we got this guy on our floor who has these tropical fish, and he had gone home for the weekend, so I was looking after them.

I went down to his room with a couple of beers. The fish tank is lit by this black light that makes the tropical fish seem to glow. I sprinkled some food on the water, then laid back on the bed. It was very soothing, watching the fish nibble at the flakes—it's almost like a drug or something, because you get very focused: there's nothing but the fish. Of course, I fell asleep.

Later I was awakened by a knock. It was early in the morning, first light. The fish were still swimming in the tank—I wonder if they ever sleep. I opened the door and Lucy stepped inside, wearing my bathrobe.

I said, Success?

Lucy smiled, and it was that beautiful smile, then she hugged me. I just want to thank you, she said, and she was even trembling a little when she added, Jerome is just the most remarkable human being I've ever met.

What happened, Father, is they took to each other the way I've never seen before. I mean it was the kind of love you dream about. Clearly, it was very spiritual, and as far as the other stuff— the physical—well, I just don't know. When they're together, they hold hands, they hug, they gaze into each other's eyes—to the point where it can get pretty boring if you're along for the ride. We went to a lot of protests together. You remember that big one on the Common? We spent the day singing and listening to speeches. And in the midst of it all Jerome and Lucy were in this quiet love-bubble. To tell you the truth, I found some of it pretty obscene. I mean, we were supposed to be protesting a war. I suppose you might think I'm jealous—and perhaps I was. Am. I don't know. But there was something about it that gave off a bad smell, too. They got to the point where they talked in a kind of code much of the time. There were Latin phrases Jerome had taught her, and they kept talking about people I didn't know. Finally I realized these were all made up. But they talked about these made up people so *convincingly*—people with names like

Miguel and Juanita and Raul. They had created an imaginary mountain village—this was where they were going to go and do missionary work.

Finally, one night Jerome and I were out on our own. It was a Thursday night and one of the priests over at the seminary had two tickets to the Bruins game that he couldn't use, so he gave them to Jerome.

We took the trolley down Comm Ave, and as we passed BU, I said, Bless me, Father, for I have sinned.

Jerome said, We haven't played that in a while.

I deceived a friend, I said. I know this seminarian who has suffered from tremendous temptation. So I conspired with a girl I know who loves to take boys down a rite of passage. I introduced them to each other, then I went off to feed the fish. Don't know what happened after that. Sometimes I think he lost his virginity and is enjoying her generosity, and sometimes I think their union is purely spiritual. When they talk about missionary work I don't think it's a euphemism.

That's what I told Jerome, Father. The trolley went underground at Kenmore Square, and he didn't speak for a while. We could see our reflections in the dark glass and occasionally the wheels threw sparks in the black tunnel.

Then Jerome said, Are you sorry for your sin?

Yes, Father, I said.

And you're willing to do penance?

Yes, Father.

Jerome nodded but he was silent again. We came up out of the tunnel, and eventually the trolley climbed onto the elevated above Causeway Street. When we pulled into the Garden, Jerome turned to me and I could see it in his eyes: we weren't playing Confession anymore. And he said, See if you can get three Hail Marys, three Our Fathers, and an Act of Contrition, and let me know.

That's what Jerome said, Father. So what do you think?

II

Bless me, Father, for I have sinned. It has been one week since my last confession. But it was incomplete. My confessions have been incomplete for some time, which in itself is a sin. I suspect you knew this. I come here each week and whisper through this grill, and perhaps you understand things just from the sound of my voice. You don't need to know my name, but you already know who I am. I'm the Icicle Wife. You know, the woman who was beaten by her husband with a heavy icicle. Everyone knows the story, right? How this man went berserk right in his driveway, nearly killing his wife with a piece of icicle that was about the length of a baseball bat. But heavier, Father. You'd never think that frozen water could weigh that much. Or that it could do that much damage. I was in Mass General for sixteen days. Over thirty stitches were necessary to close the cuts in my scalp. My face is still swollen and the bruises are still visible—I usually go out only at night, though here, to church, of course, I can wear a veil. My jaw was dislocated. Three fingers on my right hand were broken. Two ribs were cracked. These are all healing. It's the internal injuries that are worrisome, although the doctors assure me they will heal in time. But when I walk—slowly, carefully—I can feel things inside me move around in a way I've never experienced. It's as though I was gutted like a fish, and then had everything hastily stuffed back inside. The simplest bodily functions are very difficult, very painful. Despite this, my

husband is now released on bail and he's living at his sister's. It's
the way the law works. There's a restraining order which doesn't
allow him to come within a hundred feet of me. Still, I see him.
I see him in his car as he drives by the house several times a night.
Always at night. Our daughter is frightened. She's almost twelve
now. She wants me to call the police when we see his car. But I
don't, I haven't. He'd be long gone by the time any cruiser arrived. Besides I know he doesn't want to hurt me anymore. That's
not what he wants. What he wants is what's in the house. His
wife, his daughter, the furniture he sat on, the bed he slept in for
over a decade. He wants his life back. Or, perhaps I should say,
he wants the life he believed he had back. See, I stole it. I took it
away from him and his pain is only getting worse. So in a sense
I'm better off than he is. I'm on the mend—my wounds are
healing. His grow larger, deeper every day. Of course, this all has
to do with love. I've been a devout Catholic my whole life, Father, but some time ago, several years, I remember hearing you
give a sermon about love. It was a fine sermon but, with all due
respect, as I listened I said to myself, He's talking about one kind
of love. He can't know the other, because he has taken his vows.
And when I realized that, I felt sympathy for you, and also jeal-
ousy. Because you took your vows God protects you, keeps you
from knowing what we know. What men like my husband know.
What an ordinary woman with a husband and child knows. What
I know. What I found out, Father, was that one morning I got
up and realized I no longer loved the man I was married to. There
was no reason for this. He was a good man, sincere, decent, and
more honest than most, I think. And certainly he had his flaws,
as does any man. But there it was: I no longer felt love for him.
What do you do in a situation like this? I carried on, of course. I
continued to live my days as I had before. And after a while, a
good while, I realized that he had no idea how I felt. It didn't
matter whether I loved him or not. Because my behavior hadn't
changed, he had no idea that I didn't love him anymore. Essen-
tially I was living a lie. If I were a truly honest person, I would
have sat him down and said, I don't love you anymore and our

life together has to change, it has to end, it has to be different
from what it's been. But I didn't have the courage to do that.
And I've often wondered, if it had been the other way around, if
my husband had realized that he was not in love with me, what
would he do? I think he would have told me. He would sit
down and say, I don't love you. He has the strength to do that. I
don't. As a result I became angry with everything: with myself
for living this lie, with my husband for not being able to understand that I didn't love him—even though there was no way he
could have known. I was disappointed in myself and I expected
too much of him. Strangely enough it was my daughter, when
she was about ten, who began to suspect me. There was one
afternoon in particular, when we were driving in the car, going
on some errands after I had picked her up from school. I realized
that she was watching me as I was driving, and when I looked at
her I could see understanding in her eyes. She knew about my
lie. I don't know how she knew, but from her look I could tell
that she was alarmed, confused and curious, especially curious.
She's a smart child and was thinking, If she doesn't love my father, why is she doing this? I hope she wasn't also thinking, If she
doesn't love Daddy, maybe she doesn't really love me either. That
certainly isn't true. We said nothing—*I* said nothing—and did
our errands as planned. From that moment on it was like a shared
secret. There were times when I wanted to sit and talk with her
about it. Selfishly, I thought it might help me. But she was only
ten, a child. Life was confusing enough for her already. To adults
this situation may also seem confusing, but in a different way.
Father, I know that the first thing people think when they hear
about the Icicle Wife, about husbands beating their wives, is there
must be someone else. There must have been another man or,
perhaps, more than one man. They think the woman is probably
a common whore. Though some people, I think, also *want* to
believe that it's another man, just one man, and that the woman
can't help it because, for whatever reasons, she has really fallen in
love with him. These people, some of them anyway, harbor their
own longings, to be free of their lives, their marriages, their fami-

lies, and what they really feel toward that woman everyone is talking about is envy. She had the nerve to act upon her love, regardless of the consequences. Her love was that strong, that real. And they know they would give up their safe lives if they could feel that kind of love, even for only a little while. I can see it in their eyes now. These people look at me, the Icicle Wife, and there's a confusion in their eyes. They want to look away from my bruises, but they also want to assure themselves that what they've heard—the damage that was done was not exaggerated. They also want to see the love that they desire, they want to see how, even now, it helps me to bear all of the hurt, all of the embarrassment. A part of them wants to believe that I didn't deserve what I got, and that perhaps some day my love for this other man, the new life I build with him, will make all this pain worthwhile. And I assure you, Father, there was just one other man. I know that still constitutes adultery, but it is not the same as being a common whore. Just as I had gotten up one morning to discover that I no longer loved my husband, there was another morning, several years later, when I got up to discover that I felt love again. For a man, a friend of ours, a man that I saw several times in the course of a week. And slowly, over many months, I could feel something down inside me turning. It warmed and opened up, until one day it was there again, and I was so amazed—stunned is really the word—I was stunned to find out that I could *feel* love again. I know people say they can't help it, and you, Father, of course you say, But you must resist. You consider such love a temptation. What you don't understand is that when you've lost such love once, and you are convinced that you'll never feel anything like it again, and *then,* suddenly, there it is blossoming inside you again, you simply cannot resist. We are too weak—I am too weak. I was dead and it gave me my life back. And this other man, he felt the same way, and though I am here to confess, Father, I cannot deny that what we were to each other was good. We saved each other's life—I'm certain of it. But of course, my husband found out eventually. I'm not sure how, and it doesn't really matter. I believe someone else saw us together and told my husband. And here he did an odd thing: he didn't say anything to me, not at first. Instead, he went to the other man, our friend, and told him that he knew about us. The other man said he would stop seeing me immediately. He called me up and told me, and I have to tell you nothing ever hurt me so much as that phone call. I was angry that he was abandoning me. He still swore he loved me but it couldn't go on, and I was afraid—afraid of falling back into that place where I had felt no love. So that's when I confronted my husband. I was so distraught that I blamed him for stealing from me the only thing I had. It was on a Saturday morning, a day after that big blizzard we had last month. My daughter wasn't home—she had slept overnight at a friend's—and my husband was getting his coat and boots on to go out and shovel the driveway. I was sitting there in my robe, drinking coffee, thinking that this is going to be the rest of my life and I couldn't stand another minute of it. So I asked why he went to this other man, this friend, and how could he convince him to stop seeing me. I was outraged—at both men. My husband and I argued there in the front hall and all the while he kept trying to get his boots laced, his coat zipped up, his gloves and hat on—I suppose it was at that point quite comical. We went on and on and I realized that he was just trying to get away from me, to get outdoors, because he had already succeeded—succeeded in taking the love I had away from me. So I wouldn't let him go. He went out on the front porch and I followed him. We were shouting, Father, horrible things. He went down the front steps, and I followed, in my bathrobe and slippers. And as we stood in the driveway yelling we heard a rumble from above, then a loud crack. It was really very frightening. Snow slid down one of the sides of the roof and its weight broke free an enormous icicle—every winter one forms there on the north side of the house. We have to park carefully in the driveway because several years ago one of our cars got hit twice by chucks of ice that broke off. So we're standing out there in the driveway shouting, when this huge icicle crashes into the snowbank alongside the house, only a few feet from us. One of the pieces of ice—one of the smaller pieces—deflects off the snowbank and lands at my husband's feet. And he picks it up. When he straightened up with that icicle in his hands, holding it like a baseball bat, I could see that he wanted to kill me, right there in our driveway. I turned to go back into the house, but he hit me on the side of the head. I remember that first blow and falling foward into the cold snow, but I don't remember much after that. I know I begged him to stop, my arms were outstretched, but he kept on hitting me. I can see his face as he had the icicle raised above his head for another swing, and the look in his eyes was pure determination. He was killing me. This is what made me scream; it wasn't really the pain, it was the realization that he was hitting me with all he had because he wanted me dead. Nothing I could do or say would stop him, and after a point I had difficulty understanding what was happening around me, although I now know that, fortunately, one of our neighbors and his two teenaged boys were out shoveling their driveway and they came over, and it took all three of them to restrain my husband. So here I am, the woman people call the Icicle Wife. I can live with that. I have no choice. I don't know what you have in mind as penance, but now that I've told you what I have done let me tell you what I'm going to do. I've decided to ask my husband to come back into our house. I know he will because that's why he keeps driving by. I think we can live together now because he understands what happened to me—he understands that I stopped loving him and that I did the only thing I could to save myself. We have a daughter to raise, but she's not the only reason I'm doing this, though that in itself would be reason enough. I'm doing this because I think we can love each other again, my husband and I. Not as before, but as we are now, knowing what we're both capable of: I did something that hurt him deeply, and he tried to kill me. We know each other now. What more could we ask of each other? If we find love, it will only be because we know each other's heart. No one will ever see it. They'll just see the Icicle Husband and Wife, and they'll think, What a tragedy. They'll never know what we have found. They'll never know the truth.

III

Father? I can't remember the last time I went to confession and I'm not sure why I'm here now. I know I'm supposed to say Bless me, Father, for I have sinned, but the truth is I'm not sure I know what a sin is—or perhaps it would be more accurate to say I don't know what isn't a sin. It seems that to live is a sin: to walk down the street, to desire something from this life, some joy, some pleasure, and it's a sin in the eyes of the Church.

I have come to you in particular because someone said you just listen. You never question, you never probe; you just listen. When the confession is complete you give penance and say the Prayer of Absolution. I admire that. I suspect that it's extremely difficult to sit there, inches away from the faces of your parishoners, who are just voices in the dark. To listen is a great virtue, and no doubt at times it's hard to resist speaking.

As a boy I wanted to be a priest. For years I said a boy's form of mass in my home. I used one of my parents' wine glasses, and my mother gave me an old bedsheet, which I awkwardly cut into the shape of a chasuble, and with a red crayon I drew an awkward cross on the front and back. And when my grandmother died, my Irish Nana, my parents let me keep all of her religious statues in my room. There were a lot of them. I think now of that room when I was ten, eleven, and I realize how strange it was: statues of Mary, of Jesus, of Joseph, of angels and saints, crowding bookshelves and the floor and the windowsill in a boy's room. In those days I used to talk to God all the time, and on the night that Nana died, a very cold winter's night, I swear I heard angels singing. It's the only time in my life I've ever experienced anything like it. I was lying in my bed, unable to sleep, and I heard this high beautiful choir singing. I know I was awake—I wasn't dreaming. I listened for a long time, then got up the nerve to get out of bed. I went to the door of my room and looked out into the hall. My room was on the third floor—the rest of the family slept downstairs, and I could tell that everyone else was asleep. The music wasn't coming from downstairs. I went to the radiator at the end of my bed, because it would often make noise—whistle and clang and hiss in almost a ghostly fashion. But the music wasn't coming up from the heat pipes. When I got back in bed I looked out the window at the bare branches of the large maple that loomed beside our house. The music was faint and clear, but it wasn't coming from any particular direction. I looked at those branches, some glistening with a coating of ice, and listened to the angels sing—I was convinced it was angels and it had to do with the fact that my Nana had died and gone to heaven that night. I believed that, and I believed that she had requested that the angels sing for me. It was the kind of thing Nana would do.

Then for several years I was an altarboy, which at first seemed to be the appropriate step toward the priesthood. But I made a discovery about some of the priests that was disturbing: they were ordinary men. In fact, I didn't like or respect some of them. They could be bossy and cold and, at times, even mean to us altarboys. I was selected to serve at the funerals in our parish—which was something of a tribute—and the coldness was apparent in their attitude toward the families of the dead. I came to see that the priests were putting on a show, providing the families with a performance, a ritual, for which they expected to be compensated. They would come into the sacristy before a funeral—or a mass, but it was most noticeable when there was a funeral—and they would seem to be as abrupt and blunt as men going to work—it could have been any job they didn't like. They would give us orders in a way that I often resented, and some of them would even find ways of expressing dissatisfaction with us while the mass was being said. Then, after the service was over, they seemed in haste to leave the sacristy, and they were often telling us to hurry up and put things away, snuff the candles on the altar, take off our surplices and soutanes, and get across the parking lot to school. I thought the celebration of the mass would be the most important function of a priest, and I never understood their haste. They were ordinary men and I lost my admiration for them.

After sixth grade I went from St. Paul's Parochial School, to the public junior high school. Then, as a public school student, I was supposed to attend Sunday school at St. Paul's. The first year it was all right; we were taught by a young priest, a visiting seminarian, who spoke to us boys about natural temptations in a way that suggested that what we were going through wasn't extraordinary, and it wasn't necessarily bad. The second year, however, we had another young seminarian who was unable to control a roomful of fourteen-year-old boys, seated in folding wooden chairs in the basement of the church hall, and as a result he felt it was his responsibility to punish us. He used his pointer as a switch and whacked our palms or the backs of our legs. The more he did this, the more unruly we became. Then one Sunday there was a near rebellion until he made a kid named Walsh come to the front of the room and kneel on the cold concrete floor with his arms stretched out sideways in the form of a cross. Walsh remained in that position for the better part of an hour. When his arms began to sag, the priest would tap the underside of Walsh's elbow with his pointer. Walsh's back was to us, but we could see that he was in real pain, and that toward the end of class his shoulders quivered as he cried. I never went to Sunday school after that. As soon as mass was over I got as far away from the church as fast as I could, and I usually ended up in a back booth at the Sunshine Dairy drinking Coke with other boys who were skipping Sunday school.

Throughout high school I pulled further and further away from the Church. I still went to mass, but not once to Sunday school, and I discovered that my parents couldn't make me attend. Then I went to Boston College, not because it was a Catholic school but because I was a good athlete in high school and they offered me a hockey scholarship. As a freshman I got a D in theology. The old priest who taught the course was a drunk. That, I suspect, was the remedy for alcoholic Jesuits: make them teach freshman theology. We sat in long wooden benches in a cold classroom in Fulton Hall and it was like something out of the nineteenth century. The priest yammered on and on about the Trinity and Transubstantiation and the Immaculate Conception, and I always sat toward the back, reading novels and short stories, Hemingway, Fitzgerald and Joyce mostly. I realized at that point that Catholicism was for me a dead thing; something I had been raised in, but now, in early adulthood, it provided no meaningful points of reference. In principle I still believed in Christianity, that I should live a life that was decent, honest and fair. But I believed that these principles only made sense because they made civilized life possible. Without them there would be social chaos. Which, I suppose, may be the case too often. How rarely are we really civilized? As far as the Catholic church went, I wanted no more to do with it.

For years I've encountered people who felt the same way. Usually we say we were *Raised as a Catholic.* Sometimes one will jokingly refer to him or herself as a *Recovering Catholic.* I think of us as escapees. No one ever says *I'm no longer a Catholic.* After you're a convict, you're an ex-convict. It's not a past one can deny. When I was in my twenties and thirties it was not uncommon for my fellow ex-cons to seek something else, something to replace whatever it was that Catholicism used to provide. A lot of them were alcoholics. A lot of them got seriously into drugs. All of them had sex lives that the Church deemed sinful.

When I meet another ex-con I usually like that person. It seems we always have something to talk about, stories to tell about nuns and priests in our childhoods. What I find interesting about ex-cons, what we share, is that we're sinners, and yet we continue to try and live lives that are decent, honest, fair and kind. At certain points in our lives we may have lied, we may have stolen, we may have committed adultery, we may have committed sins that we know we should confess; yet we don't, and the next day we manage to go out and do something fair and decent. We discover that we are not bad people; we are just people trying to live our lives. This is such a strange sacrament, confession. To come here and kneel in the dark; to whisper what we've been taught are our sins to a priest, another human; then to be given absolution and penance. To clean the slate of our souls, as the nuns used to tell us, so that should we die before our next confession we will go to heaven because we are in the State of Grace.

Let's presume that I will die this week. I'm not old, but I'm no longer young. I could be in an accident, I could take a fall. There could be a tumor in my body that has gone undetected. My heart could stop. Still, I wouldn't know what to tell you now, what to confess. I can't find the words to describe my sins. And yet I'm here. I'm here and willing to listen. Is there anything there beyond your silence? If so, I wish you would say so, because I am here.

Snow

When I was in high school, I was blind for a day. The program was called Helping Hand, and in preparation for the arrival of several blind students the other volunteers and I had to spend one entire school day blindfolded. From homeroom through all seven periods of classes we had to keep the blindfold on and get around school without anyone's assistance. After being blind-folded, each of us was given a cane.

At first it was fun. Inching along the walls toward Mrs. Zebriski's biology class I was pleased at how clearly I could visu-alize in my mind where I was going. And the other students who passed me in the hall kidded me, telling me to "Watch out!" and "Look where you're going!" I could recognize some voices and I'd call people by their names, saying in a tough voice, "I'll see you later. Outside." In class I couldn't really participate, so it was like I was present and absent at the same time. It was like I was invisible. Only Mr. Scanlon, my civics teacher, called on me to answer a question, and it was easy, something to do with the separation of powers in the federal government.

But lunch in the cafeteria was frustrating. I got in line with my tray without any problem, and I selected my food by smell— I took the American chop suey over the tuna boat plate and the sloppy joe—however, eating blind wasn't easy. My fork kept missing my mouth, and though I wiped my lips and chin I was sure that my face was still smeared with chop suey sauce. When I left the cafeteria, a boy's voice I didn't recognize said, "Nice shirt, spaz." In the lavatory I hid in a stall, lifted the blindfold off my eyes and cleaned the food from my shirt and pants.

Afternoon classes were a pain. There was a pop quiz in trig

and we watched a film, *The Oxbow Incident,* in English. How was I supposed to go home and write an essay about a film I had only heard? Finally back in homeroom, I removed the blindfold. The lights were too bright and the other kids stared at me with dumb, expectant smiles on their faces. I turned to Colin McElroy, one of the wimpiest kids in the class, and said, "What're you starin' at?" And nobody looked at me any longer.

At basketball practice I took foul shots for over half an hour. I was incredible, hitting eight and nine out of every ten. But I remained in a bad mood and for the next couple of days nobody dared asked me about being blind.

When the real blind kids arrived—there were eight of them, five boys and three girls—I was assigned to Byron Penney, from Leominster. Byron had straight greasy black hair, severe acne, and he wore loud striped shirts without collar buttons. He didn't wear sunglasses like some of the other blind kids and the skin around his nearly shut eyes was dark and aged. I "showed" Byron around Cotton Mather High, walking him to all his classes, to his locker, to the cafeteria, to the lavatory and to the gym, where Byron, who was in reasonable shape, did calisthenics on the wrestling mats while the rest of the phys-ed class played basketball. I assisted Byron for three days, as I was supposed to; then I checked up with him each Monday morning for the next two weeks, as I was supposed to, making sure that Byron was getting around all right.

Actually Byron was a good kid. He loved basketball and he never missed a broadcast of a Celtics' game—if you closed your eyes you'd swear his impression of announcer Johnny Most was the real thing. But he was a blind kid and after not too many weeks I no longer checked on him, even to the point where when I passed him in the halls between classes I wouldn't say anything—like most of the other students at Cotton Mather High. And sometimes in the cafeteria I would see Byron at another table, getting food on his face and clothes. He usually sat with other blind students.

In late February at the end of the basketball team's regular season I found a note tucked in my locker door: "Great season! I listened to all your games on the radio. Best luck in the State Tournament—Byron." I felt proud—I had a fan. But I also felt selfish and ashamed. During the week that the team practiced for the first round of the tourney, I imagined doing something for Byron. Bringing him on the team bus to the state champion-ship game. Or when interviewed by a sports reporter, dedicating a win to Byron Penney. Or getting the other players to make him an official member of the team, allowing him to sit on the bench with us, wearing a Frigates' jersey and holding a portable radio to his ear so he could listen to Johnny Most's special broadcast of the championship game. Of course Johnnie Most didn't broad-cast the championship game and I didn't do any of these things for Byron, but I imagined them in lengthy and vivid detail every afternoon at practice while I took my foul shots.

Over the next couple of weeks the Cotton Mather Frigates moved through the field of contenders in the state tournament and lost the championship game. Afterwards I was bitter. I'd played well and we lost. I deserved better. We were that close. I rarely thought about Byron Penney, and once when I passed the blind kid tapping his way down the hall I thought, "I don't owe him anything. It's his tough luck he's blind. It's not my fault."

I tried not to think about Byron Penney after that. Such thoughts were cruel and I knew I shouldn't have them.

Some winters in New England never seem to go away. That March was colder than January and February; it broke records set back in the last century. The last weekend of the month there was a dance at school, in the gymnasium, which was decorated with crepe, tinfoil and colored lights. The theme was April Fool's so the principal, Mr. Delveccio, was wearing a jester's outfit, com-plete with bells on the curled-up toes of his shoes. The band was lousy. Not many kids had come because of the weather. The dance was a dud.

I was pretty drunk. Since basketball season had ended I'd been drunk every weekend. It was something I'd been promising my-self all winter, but now that I was out of training, being drunk didn't have that much appeal. It made me remorseful and sometimes it made me throw up. I didn't like being in the gym with all the decorations hanging from the ceiling and backboards, trying to conceal the fact that we were on a basketball court; I kept remembering the home games that winter and I'd stand in a spot and think, "I hit that jumper against Agawam North from right here. I was unconscious that night."

I only stayed an hour at the dance and was about to leave when Mrs. Delveccio, who was divorced from Mr. Delveccio and was a guidance counselor at school, came up to me with Byron Penney close to her side. She was wearing a red gown that was supposed to suggest that she was a queen, and Byron was wearing an ordinary blue Oxford button-down collar shirt like just about every guy at Cotton Mather owned. But there was something wrong. He was pale and sweaty, and he was walking funny. Byron Penney was drunk. Mrs. Delveccio explained to me that his uncle, who was supposed to pick Byron up, had skidded off an icy section of the Mass Turnpike and she wondered if Byron could stay at my house for the night. I told her sure, no problem.

When she left us Byron said, "I asked Lorraine Newman to dance with me to 'Mustang Sally.' I'll bet she was something. I can tell by a girl's voice what kind of dancer she is."

He was trying to make me feel guilty. I was sure of it. "Nice shirt," I said.

Byron's hand quickly came up and felt the front of his shirt.

"It's clean," I said.

"What's wrong with it then?"

"It's a button-down."

"So? Where does it say that I can't wear it?"

"Don't get so defensive." I looked away for a moment. I was drunk and Byron was drunk. We were getting into an argument, and I knew that there was no way I could win. That was feeling sorry for the guy. That's what I hated about dealing with Byron. If it were anybody else, I could just cut him down. Then I said, "Byron, why don't you wear sunglasses like the others?"

Byron didn't answer. He faced me, his head tilted up too high, as always. His lips began to tremble. "I didn't want to come to this damned school, and I didn't want to stay for this dance. Now my uncle's car is stuck in a snowbank somewhere and I've got to spend the night with this basketball asshole who thinks he's big stuff." Byron was crying and he turned and started to walk away, tapping his cane ahead of him so other kids would get out of his way. "Coming through!" he said loudly over the music. "Blind drunk coming through!" He moved so quickly that some kids didn't have time to get out of his way and he bumped into them, backed up, then bumped into someone else.

I couldn't believe I'd caused it. Finally I went after Byron, grabbed him by the arm and led him out of the gym.

We stopped in the boys' lavatory because Byron had to throw up. He said he felt better after that.

"You ever drink Colt .45?" he asked as we got our overcoats.

"Yeah."

"Stinks, doesn't it?"

"Naragansett's worse." I opened the door for Byron and we went out into the cold. "Lorraine Newman is a pretty good dancer, but you should see Lucinda Knapp."

"You ever get anywhere with her?"

I shook my head. Then I said, "No."

We got in my father's Oldsmobile, and I drove slowly because of the ice. Byron and I didn't talk so I turned on the radio. The Bruins game was on. "I hate hockey," I said as I reached for the knob to find some music.

"I listen to any game I can find on the radio," Byron said. "The radio is freedom. I turn it on and the world gets wide, you know? Home games from Boston Garden are one thing, but away games! Detroit and Chicago—they're so far away. There's all that distance."

I left the hockey game on. The announcer was talking about how fast the ice was tonight at Montreal Forum. Reaching under the driver's seat I pulled out my last bottle of beer and gave it and a church key to Bryon. He opened it, drank some and passed the bottle back to me. "What is that?"

"Pickwick Ale," I said. The liquid was partially frozen from sitting in the car. It hardly had any flavor, only a burning sensation on the tongue.

"It's different."

"Just give it a few minutes."

Byron reached across toward me and I placed the bottle in his hand.

"I got an idea," I said. "I want to show you something before we go home."

Byron placed his other hand over his eyes and pretended to peek through spread fingers. Sliding down in the seat, he said, "This I gotta see."

I drove out to Hawthorne Lake on the edge of town and pulled over on a dark section of Algonquin Road.

"If we're going parking," Byron said, "I'm not that kind of girl."

"Come on, get out."

"'Blind boy left to freeze in cold and dark,'" he said in a deep voice. "'High school prank suspected. Details at eleven.'"

"Leave your cane in the car," I said.

It was very cold and the air was still. There was a perfect silence. I took Byron's arm and walked him out onto the lake, which was frozen and covered with about a half foot of snow.

"Before you came they made all us Helping Handers go around school blindfolded for a day," I said.

"It's a blast, isn't it?"

"I cheated once."

"I tried that too but I couldn't live with myself afterwards." He gave me the bottle. "Where are we, somewhere out in the open?"

"Hawthorne Lake." I let go of his arm and he stopped. I kept going, and after a moment he caught up. We continued across the lake, shoulder to shoulder. I could feel him trying to slow down, but I kept my normal pace.

"You been this way since birth?" I asked.

"Yeah. My mother drank a fifth a day and I came out singing 'Oh Danny Boy.'"

I took a swig of ale and passed the bottle back to him.

"Don't you hate it? I mean, sometimes doesn't it just—I don't know."

"The other day I got called down to the guidance office and they were sitting there, Mrs. Delveccio and Father Helping Hand himself, and they asked me how I was doing. I could tell by their voices that it was going to be one of those occasions: the moment for a big decision. They wanted to know if I wanted to come back to Cotton Mather High for senior year, or—" Byron stopped short.

The ice had boomed, echoing dully through the surrounding hills. Under the snow we could hear the ice crackle and ping as it settled.

"It's at least a foot thick," I said. We started walking again. "Cotton Mather or?"

"Or this private school out in the Berkshires that has a special program for the blind." He gave me the bottle again. "I asked them if it was co-ed. They said no, and I said no. I like being around girls. I can smell them all day long, in class, in the halls."

"You know I'd pass you in the hall and I wouldn't say anything."

Byron stopped again. His shoulders sagged and he let out a sigh. "Oh!" He reached out and found my shoulders with his hands and clutched them. "I'm *so* glad you told me!" he shouted. He dropped his arms to his sides and took a deep breath. "Now I can tell you," he gasped. "I don't know *how* many times I passed you in the halls and pretended not to smell you."

I gave him the beer bottle. "Finish it."

Drinking, he raised his head to the dark winter sky. He gave back the empty bottle. "It's beginning to snow," he said.

I turned my face upwards and felt the first light, cool touch of snow.

"There's really only one thing I've ever wanted to see," Byron said. "Well, all right, there's two—but one of them's snow. What's it look like?"

I looked up into the darkness again. I couldn't see the snow either, only feel it. "I have no idea how to answer that."

"I understand every snowflake is different. Once in a chemistry class we made crystals and the teacher said they were like snow. I felt them with my fingers—they had sharp edges and a kind of symmetry. Another time, when I was little, we cut snowflakes out of newspaper, and their shape was determined by what we cut away before unfolding the paper."

"Byron, I'm basically a dumb jock. I've seen snow all my life and I can't describe it better than that."

He stepped closer to me. "Why'd you bring me out here?"

I couldn't remember exactly.

Byron shook his head. "Jeez, you *are* pretty thick. Better hope you have another good basketball season if you want to get into college."

"I just remembered why I brought you out here."

"Yeah?"

"I thought you might want to be in the middle."

Byron stood with his head raised as if he were trying to identify a smell. Then he ran, just ran as hard and fast as he could, zigzagging and jumping and skidding on the snow, his shouts and laughter coming back to me in the dark.

Other books by John Smolens

Winter By Degrees

Angel's Head

**Carnegie Mellon University Press
Series in Short Fiction**

Fortune Telling
David Lynn

A New and Glorious Life
Michelle Herman

The Long and Short of It
Pamela Painter

The Secret Names of Woman
Lynne Barrett

The Law of Return
Maxine Rodburg

The Drowning and Other Stories
Edward Delaney

My One and Only Bomb Shelter
John Smolens

Very Much Like Desire
Diane Lefer